Ivy knew she given a one-way ticket out of Rick's life

Rick wiped his paint-stained hands, then said, "There's a whole new dimension to relationships in which the rules are constantly changed. Usually by the female."

"Rick..." she began.

He ignored her. "And woe be unto him who fails to *notice* when those rules change, making lustful overtures not only in bounds, but expected."

Ivy ducked her head, but Rick tipped up her chin, compelling her to meet his eyes. "And what happens to the woman?"

Ivy smiled. A tiny, hopeful, daring smile. "She gets kissed?"

"Only if she agrees the rules have changed." Rick looked at her in a way he hadn't before, in the way Ivy had often hoped he would. "*Have* they changed?"

Dear Reader,

It took me longer to write the last chapter of *Ivy's League* than any other chapter because typing "The End" meant saying goodbye to Holly, Laurel and Ivy—and Adam, Jack and Rick.

The Hall sisters have been with me a long time. The baby whose Christmas colic attack inspired Holly's story, *Deck the Halls,* is now in first grade.

In *Jack of Hearts,* Laurel had to learn to play poker, which meant *I* had to learn to play poker. The year I wrote the book, both my husband and dad traveled frequently on business. When their trips coincided, I invited my mom and sister over for an all-night poker party. We needed more players and included my two gleeful sons. We weren't very good, but we had a lot of fun. As I recall, the boys won with some of the most incredible hands ever dealt. They swear they didn't cheat.

Flush with success—and chips—the boys eagerly offered to help with *Ivy's League.* They signed up for baseball, T-ball, swimming and soccer so I could try out sports for Ivy. Soccer won and they still play. Fiction became reality last season when I encountered the same situation that confronted an exasperated Ivy—we had a team and no coach. The parents were told that one of us had to volunteer or the team would disband. As I looked around for an Ivy-like person, I kept thinking, "This can't be happening—I made it up!" By the way, one of the dads coached and the team won every game.

So, rather than saying goodbye to the Hall sisters, I'll check in on them from time to time, especially to watch Nicholas grow up. After all, with Adam for a father and Jack and Rick as uncles, how can he become anything other than a Harlequin hero?

Sincerely,

Heather Allison

IVY'S LEAGUE
Heather Allison

Harlequin Books

TORONTO • NEW YORK • LONDON
AMSTERDAM • PARIS • SYDNEY • HAMBURG
STOCKHOLM • ATHENS • TOKYO • MILAN
MADRID • WARSAW • BUDAPEST • AUCKLAND

To my Alpha Gamma Delta sisters
Special red and buff roses to the
Houston Alumnae Club
And to Linda Freise Proch,
a true blue old chum

ISBN 0-373-03269-2

Harlequin Romance first edition June 1993

IVY'S LEAGUE

CHAPTER ONE

" 'MEN IN GENERAL are but great children.' Napoleon said that. Write it down."

Ivy Hall dutifully scribbled the quote in her reporter's notebook as Billie White, a local free-lance photographer, continued. "Look at them." Billie gestured at the practice field near the University of Texas campus where the Longhorns' season-opening opponent scrimmaged. "The temperature's 102 in the shade, if you could find any shade, and those boys are out there knocking themselves silly." She rested her ankle on one knee and propped her elbow on the other. Billie worked hard to maintain her hard-bitten, I've-seen-it-all image.

Ivy shifted on the hot aluminum bench and squinted into the afternoon sun. "The Colts have to practice somewhere." She grinned. "Not that practice will do them any good." Ivy, like all true Texas Exes, had burnt-orange blood flowing through her veins, inspiring a fierce loyalty to her alma mater, the University of Texas.

"Sure it will," Billie replied. "Male bonding. You know, 'a mystic bond of brotherhood makes all men one'? You gotta remember that." Billie pointed to Ivy's notebook. "Carlyle." Ivy wrote, because she didn't want to hurt the feelings of the eccentric photographer, who was something of an institution at Austin-area football games.

"Underline it."

"Billie . . ."

"I'm serious."

Ivy, with an exasperated look, underlined Carlyle's quote. Twice.

"You think I'm crazy, don't you?"

Maybe a little. "I don't think men are engaged in a conspiracy against us," Ivy said, sidestepping Billie's question.

"No? What are you doing right now?"

"Sitting here watching the Colts practice."

"That's 'cause, besides me, nobody's talking to you." Billie nodded to the scattered groups of men clustered around the entrance to the locker room, the players' bench, the first rows of the bleachers and the assistant coaches. "We're up here. The action's down there. Now that's not so bad for me—" Billie patted her telephoto lens "—but you've gotta hustle for *your* story."

"I plan to interview the team after the scrimmage."

"Where?"

"The locker room."

Billie lifted one of the cameras slung around her neck and peered through the viewfinder. "You a cub reporter, honey?"

"I've been with the *Austin Globe* since June." And was thrilled to be with the weekly sports newspaper. Ivy had wanted to be a sports reporter for as long as she could remember. Working for a weekly publication entirely devoted to sports was her idea of heaven.

"Two months. You're a cub."

"But I interned with the *Lone Star*." And hadn't liked it. Too much pressure on a daily paper.

Down came the camera. "Surprised you didn't learn more."

"What don't I know?"

"Beans." Billie shook her head. "You don't know beans. Look at you."

Involuntarily, Ivy looked down at herself, causing her sunglasses to slide to the end of her nose. Irritated, she shoved them back into place. "I'm wearing pants and a shirt. What's wrong with that?"

"Miss Preppie of the Year. Your shirt has that little horseback rider on it and it's white."

"What's wrong with white?"

"You can see through white when it gets wet."

"So I won't get wet."

Billie snorted. "I bet you even ironed your pants."

Ivy had. "I was trying for a casual professionalism." She tried not to imply that Billie's clothes suggested she was a resistance fighter. For the losing side.

"And that hair." Billie picked up a strand of Ivy's long sable brown hair. "Cut it."

"I will not!" Ivy tossed her head, sending the lock of hair rippling over her shoulders.

"You look too much like a girl."

"I *am* a girl! Woman," she amended.

"Girl. The hair goes—make a note of that. The name, too."

Ivy wiped sweat from under her sunglasses. "What's wrong with my name?"

"Gotta change it. Too feminine. If you want to get respect in this profession, you can't be feminine."

Ivy tried to curb her impatience. The idea that female sports reporters had to imitate men was such an outdated issue. "Male fashion reporters aren't expected to wear heels and makeup."

"Then how come so many of 'em do?"

"Billie!"

"They're not fooling anybody by calling it bronzing gel. Decide on a name yet?"

Ivy had no intention of changing anything about her appearance or her name. She was a full-time professional—finally. And she was going to act like one. "Too bad my parents didn't name me Billie."

Billie chuckled. "I wasn't *named* Billie. Real name's Wilma. What can we do with Ivy? Ivy...Ivy...Ivan? No, you don't look Russian. Sissy name, anyway. What's your middle name?"

"Christine."

"Chris! Perfect—an all-American name! From now on, you're Chris."

"Billie," Ivy began, not wanting to insult the well-meaning photographer. The woman wore army fatigues and a shapeless jacket, with a baseball cap on her head. Her gray-streaked hair was cut about ear length, probably by Billie herself. Billie could have been a man or a woman. "I'd like to try it my way first. I know that when you started in sports twenty years ago—"

"Thirty."

"Thirty years ago, there was a lot of resentment for female sports reporters—"

"Still is, honey."

"But we're all professionals now, and I think the coaches and players realize that. We're just doing our jobs."

"So why're you stuck up here listening to my war stories when the other reporters are on the field interviewing the opposing team's coach?"

Ivy glanced at the players' bench. The opening game of the fall football season was this weekend. The other squad, Texas Central State, was a good-size school, but the University of Texas was favored to win, as usual.

"Bud and I are splitting the interviews and will pool our information later."

"Is that what he told you?"

Ivy nodded.

"And you believed him?"

Ivy nodded again. "I've pooled information before."

"With *that* bunch? In sports?"

"Bud is new, too. And when we were in college—"

Billie was shaking her head as Ivy spoke. "You poor baby. Listen to Mama, honey."

Ivy had a feeling she didn't want to hear this. She suspected she'd once again been naive and gullible, and she hated that about herself. She wasn't a child, didn't think she acted like a child, but Holly and Laurel, her two older sisters, had always treated her like a child.

Ivy had been fourteen when her parents were killed in a plane crash. Since then, her sisters had left her out of all major discussions. They had protected her—for her own good, of course. She couldn't help being the baby of the family, but she'd show them she'd finally grown up. And she'd show them by becoming a successful, financially independent, sportswriter.

"Chris, my child," Billie began, and Ivy winced. "You are being scooped as we speak." Billie pointed to Ivy's former classmate, now a reporter for one of the Austin dailies. "Bud may be new, but he's becoming chums with those coaches. Then tomorrow after the game, who are they going to talk to? You? Or their good pal Bud? Are they going to say, 'Hey, Chris, how about a beer?'"

Ivy shook her head, never mind that her name wasn't Chris. "I don't like beer."

"'Eat, drink and be merry,'" quoted Billie.

"'For tomorrow we shall—'"

Billie elbowed her. "You don't need to write that last part."

Ivy grinned. "I wasn't going to write the first part."

"Suit yourself. You'll see. You're too nice."

"I know."

"You need to be more aggressive."

"I know." Ivy sighed.

"If you aren't aggressive, you'll never get good stories."

"I *know*."

"In fact, you need to sashay right down to that locker room, and when the players come in from practice, nab the most promising one and ask him what he considers his team's chances are for beating the Longhorns."

"I thought you were a photographer." But Billie wasn't telling Ivy anything she hadn't told herself. This was her first field assignment for the *Globe*. She was nervous. She had retreated to the bleachers to gather her thoughts, review her questions. "Anyway, I'll be okay. Being female will work to my advantage. I'll be noticed. Wouldn't the players rather talk to me than to some out-of-shape ex-jock reliving past glories?"

She stood, preparing to find a place—preferably out of the merciless August sun—where she could wait and single out a player.

"Now where are you going?" Billie asked.

"To the locker room." Ivy tossed off the information as if she hadn't been dreading this moment ever since she'd accepted the assignment.

"Do you think they're going to let you in the locker room?"

"After ten minutes, if they admit anyone else, they have to let me in. It's the law."

"Did you ever think they can make it so you won't want to go in there?"

Of course she had. Constantly. "Harassment is illegal."

Billie eyed her with an expression that told Ivy her naïveté was showing. "What are you going to do the first time a player drops his towel? Or doesn't bother with one?"

"Maintain very good eye contact."

"Uh-huh. I got a couple of stories I want you to hear."

Ivy reluctantly sat on the bleachers again. Billie had better be quick because the players were running laps. Practice was nearly over.

"Remember, 'We must laugh at man to avoid crying for him.' Napoleon again. You gonna write that down?"

"Yes, Billie."

Billie sprinkled her coarse tales with quotes and salty language. Ivy gritted her teeth and tried not to blush, tried to act as though she weren't embarrassed and tried not to look around to see if they were being overheard.

"...and you know what it was?" Billie paused expectantly.

Ivy managed a small smile. "His—" she gestured vaguely with her hands "—you know."

Billie chortled. "You can't even say—"

"I don't think I'll need to!" Ivy, blushing furiously, decided she'd had enough. She gathered her notebook and stood.

Billie grabbed her arm. "Take it easy. I'm not making fun of you. You have brothers?"

"Two sisters," Ivy mumbled.

"I could tell," Billie said, releasing Ivy's arm. "The guys are heading for the showers. Good luck, Chris."

"Oh, no!" Ivy clambered over the bleachers and sprinted toward the locker room. She'd missed staking out a place because she'd been listening to stories about male body parts. If she didn't watch it, she'd end up doing a human-interest article about Billie instead of her first hard sports story for the *Globe*.

She reached the locker room as the last of the football players retreated inside.

She waited with the other reporters until they were admitted and was immediately assailed by the pungent odor of male sweat. Water hissed and steamy fog rolled around the beige-tiled partition that divided the showers from the rest of the locker room.

Legally, she could walk right up to the showers, but Ivy chose to respect the players' privacy by waiting in the dressing area. She hoped they would recognize her courtesy and reward her with some good quotes for her article.

She glanced at her notebook, filled with Billie's bizarre quotations about men, and flipped to a clean page.

This wasn't Ivy's first locker-room trip, but it was the first time she'd approached college players.

They were much more intimidating than the junior high basketball teams.

"Hall!" Bud made his way through the crowded locker room. "Whatcha got?"

Ivy smiled nervously. "Nothing yet."

"Hey, we've been here an hour."

Ivy straightened, clutching her notebook to her chest. She'd noticed that Bud's shirt was clinging damply to him and realized her white knit was clinging damply to her. "Wait a few minutes and I'll have some info for you."

He gestured dismissively. "Forget it. I'm on deadline. I'll make do with the coaches' interviews."

"What about me?" Billie's warning reverberated through Ivy's mind.

Bud winked. "Better get busy." He waved and whistled as he strode out of the damp, smelly locker room.

Bud had duped her. Ivy the gullible. Okay, so she'd made a mistake. She wouldn't make the same one again.

She took a deep breath, regretting it instantly. The dressing area was deserted, but noisy. The reporters, coaches and players were behind the tiled wall. Ivy could hear the rumble of male laughter. Male bonding.

Males getting stories for their nine-o'clock deadlines.

A few of the nonplayers trickled out into the dressing room. The men either ignored her or stared, then laughed among themselves.

She was limp with relief—and humidity—when the first towel-clad player strolled from the showers to the lockers.

"Ivy Hall, with the *Globe,*" she announced as she approached him. "What will be your strategy against the Longhorns on Saturday?"

The Colt player toweled his hair. "To win."

"What do you consider the Longhorns' greatest weakness?"

He threw the towel on the floor right next to her feet. "Nosy women reporters."

Ivy didn't waste time with a retort. Other players were returning from the showers, along with the reporters. She glanced around to see if there were any other women. There weren't.

"Hi. You belong to anybody?" A male voice asked on her right.

Ivy whirled around, notebook at the ready. "The *Globe.*"

"A woman of the world. I like the sound of that." The beefy player leaned closer.

"Hey!" barked an older man in a navy blue Colt shirt. "We don't allow girlfriends in the locker room."

"I'm Ivy Hall, with the *Austin Globe.*" She pointed to her press pass.

The man closed his eyes. "Lord save us from women's lib."

Ivy swallowed and asked, "What's your strategy for Saturday?"

"On Saturday afternoon," he spoke slowly, watching as Ivy scribbled, "we are going to beat the—" Ivy stopped writing "—out of the Longhorns." He grinned.

"Can you be more specific?"

The question, phrased just that way, was a mistake. Ivy knew it as soon as she heard the words leave her mouth.

"Why, certainly." With a grin, the man proceeded to detail in precise and blistering language exactly what his team intended to do to the University of Texas Longhorns.

Willing away any blushes, Ivy kept her expression blank. She and this moronic coach were the center of attention. She was surrounded by large, moist males in various stages of undress.

Not a pretty sight.

"Did you get all that, hon?"

"Just need your name." Ivy's lips curved upward. Inside, she trembled.

"You should know."

She should, but the Colts had several coaches and trainers. Ivy scanned his shirt for a name embroidered anywhere on it.

"Hey, Coach Collin," a voice hollered from the other side of the room.

"Be right there," the man answered, and walked off without looking at Ivy.

The head coach. Wonderful. "Thank you for the quote, Coach Collin," she called after him.

Then she pretended to jot down a few more notes. Strands of hair stuck to her damp face. She brushed them aside, glancing up to decide which group of players to approach next.

Those few who met her gaze hastily turned away.

Great. With their coach so obviously not considering her worth his time, none of the players would speak to her now. Ivy stared resentfully after the uncouth man and saw that he was arguing with a lone player.

"I don't want to see you taking stupid chances like that on Saturday. You may be—" The coach broke off at Ivy's approach. "Listen, lady, I said all I intend to say to you." He glanced at the young man. "*I* call the plays. If you can't handle that, we'll start Brett Saturday afternoon."

Ivy had started to protest, but instead, her reporter's instinct alerted, took two steps back and hoped they'd forget she was there.

"You wouldn't," the Colt player thundered. "Not if you want a chance of winning!"

Ivy wrote surreptitiously. The Colt's quarterback... TaylorBrown. Controversy with head coach Sonny Collin?

Coach Collin lowered his voice. Ivy strained to hear. "I know you need the stats and I know you need the numbers, but the team's win-loss record is more important than your long-shot at the Heisman!''

"Not to me!'' Taylor shouted. "I'm doing more for this two-bit school than it's doing for me!''

Coach Collin jabbed Taylor's shoulder with his index finger. "And *that* attitude is why Brett might start Saturday!'' He stormed past Ivy, who immediately moved to confront the angry quarterback.

"How will this affect your already slim chances for the Heisman?''

Taylor's bare chest heaved as he gazed at the retreating coach.

The knot of players that had gathered around drifted away now that the shouting was over. Some of the other reporters left, ready to write their stories and make their deadlines. Ivy was just about to get her story. If she could find a new angle... "How will this affect your chances for the Heisman?'' she repeated.

"Huh?'' The quarterback said absently. "He's going to play me. He knows he has to.''

"He mentioned another player.'' Ivy mentally ran through the team's roster. "Brett Carson? He has some pretty impressive stats for a junior.'' Sports statistics were Ivy's speciality. The numbers always stuck with her until she needed them. "Six-two, 190, redshirted his freshman year, seven touchdown passes—''

"Hey, he had a couple of okay games while my shoulder healed. But I'm in great shape now. And I'm number one.''

"Are you?''

The Colts' quarterback stared at her, as if noticing her for the first time. His gaze flicked over her body, lingering insultingly.

"Yeah. I'm the best." Then he dropped his towel. "What do you think?"

Ivy maintained eye contact like crazy as a roaring filled her ears. It was the pounding of blood as her heart fueled the world's most gigantic blush. But before the redness could seep into her cheeks, Ivy thought of Billie and her stories and decided to borrow one.

Slowly, she forced herself to look down Taylor Brown's naked body, counted to five, then allowed her gaze to drift upward until her eyes met his. "Looks like a p—" Ivy couldn't believe she was actually saying the word "—only smaller."

The room exploded into raucous laughter. The Colts' quarterback blushed. With a furious glare at her, he grabbed his towel and bolted for the showers.

Ivy's stomach had quivered, but her voice hadn't. She could breathe again. *What do you think?* he'd asked. She thought he was a stupid clod. At this moment, she thought all men were stupid clods.

Sending a silent thanks to Billie, Ivy turned toward the door, her gaze meeting the amused brown eyes of a tall man leaning against the doorjamb, hands shoved in his pockets. He wore a jacket and tie, and unlike most of the other nonplayers she'd seen today, his stomach didn't roll over his belt. In fact, even fully clothed, he was more compelling than the brawny half-naked men surrounding her.

Her breath caught as he lazily scanned her body, imitating her encounter with the quarterback. The blush she'd been able to suppress before now fired her cheeks.

The corner of his mouth tilted in a sardonic half smile as he shook his head slightly and withdrew to the outer dressing area.

All the self-confidence she'd felt at holding her own with the quarterback evaporated with the man's obvious dismissal.

Something about him tweaked her memory. Ivy reached the doorway and watched as he sauntered through the room. He moved with the grace of an athlete—an injured one, she noted, as she saw the slight catch in his gait. Maybe he was a commentator with a television station. He had the looks for it, but not the hair. His was styled short on top, but long at the back, as if he'd changed his mind during a haircut. Golden highlights streaked through the light brown layers and Ivy knew they'd been bleached by the sun, not chemicals.

Who was he? Ivy was certain she'd seen him before, but was she supposed to recognize him?

Actually, she didn't care whether or not she was supposed to recognize him. No man was going to look at her the way he had and then just walk off. She scanned the room to see if Billie or someone else she knew was nearby. No one.

When she looked back, the man had been accosted by another reporter. Well, she was a reporter, too, wasn't she? Why shouldn't she do a little accosting of her own?

At that moment, his gaze caught hers and held it.

HE'D ALMOST ESCAPED.

The last thing Rick Scott wanted to do was talk to his newest *Globe* colleague, especially after what he'd just witnessed.

He'd watched as she'd interviewed—or tried to interview—the Colts. She'd used a good line, one he'd heard before. It would've been more effective, though, if her knees hadn't been shaking. He supposed she had potential, but she'd need a lot of seasoning before she could hold her own in a locker room.

Pity. He was too busy to play nursemaid to cub reporters.

Even slender, doe-eyed ones.

Rick made a slight movement, and the garrulous sportscaster with him grabbed his arm, preventing his escape.

Great. Now she was coming over, probably to whine and complain about how she was treated.

He didn't want to hear it. And he shouldn't have to hear it. She'd known exactly what she was getting into when she took this job. Laws or not, she'd entered a predominantly male domain and she'd better learn to handle her own problems.

He scowled at her and turned his attention back to the sportscaster—a talking dog, as they were nicknamed. Cuffing the man on the shoulder, Rick smiled and moved away, hoping the *Globe*'s new reporter wouldn't follow him.

"Excuse me."

Rick winced. His back was to her. If he kept walking, maybe she'd go away.

"Excuse me." Louder. Her voice was deep and soft, with a slight huskiness.

He felt himself weaken and sucked in a long breath. "Yeah? What is it?" He glanced over his shoulder, but kept walking.

Good grief, it was Bambi. With big brown...wounded eyes.

"I'm Ivy Hall, from the *Globe*." She had to jog to keep up with him, but he didn't feel like slowing down. Maybe she'd give up before they reached the stadium stairs. His throbbing knee was telling him he'd *have* to slow down then.

"Hey! I'm talking to you!"

Rick stopped. The stairs were a few yards ahead, anyway. "So?" He didn't turn around.

"Ivy Hall—"

"I heard." She walked around until she faced him. He wished she wouldn't stare. He shouldn't have stopped. "What do you want?" Since he was annoyed with himself, he spoke with an unintended harshness.

She blinked—a slow blink that wasn't quick enough to hide the flash of hurt.

Rick groaned. "Look, don't worry. I'll give you enough information for a story. Just don't make a big deal out of this."

She gave him a puzzled glance and shook her head, sending a wave of brown rippling behind her. "I wasn't going to ask you for a story. I've got one. But I would like to know—"

"You're going to write about Taylor Brown?" Rick interrupted.

Her quick nod confirmed his guess. She was going to shred poor Taylor in print.

Rick shoved a hand into his pocket. "Hey, the kid is under a lot of pressure. You were kind of hard on him."

"*I* was hard on him?" Her eyes glittered. "You saw what he did."

"Yeah, I saw. He got chewed out by his coach and there you were, moving right in. You caught some fall-out, okay?"

"That's no excuse."

"No, but it's a reason. Taylor is inexperienced, and I remember how I felt when reporters swarmed around me. Sometimes I just wanted—'' Rick stopped, but he was too late.

What was the matter with him? *He* was a reporter now. He hadn't played pro football in three years.

''Wanted to what?''

Rick looked down at her. She wasn't a very big person. Rather slight, with those soft brown eyes that invited you to confide. He relaxed as his anger faded. Maybe she'd do okay as a reporter, after all.

''I just wanted to be left alone.'' That wasn't what he'd been about to say and they both knew it.

''You look alone at the moment.''

He bent forward until her Bambi eyes were inches away. ''And I *like* being alone!'' As they'd talked, Rick had edged toward the stairs. Now he quickly turned away from her and started down them.

On the first step, his leg buckled and he collapsed against the handrail, the breath hissing between his teeth as pain ripped through his knee.

And then she was there, positioning herself ahead of him on the stairs, supporting him as he regained his balance. She was surprisingly strong, he discovered when he briefly leaned against her to straighten his burning knee. ''Thanks.'' He glanced at her as he spoke, dreading the pity he knew he'd see.

It wasn't there.

''The wheelchair-access ramp is one entrance down. Can you walk that far?'' Her voice was calmly neutral. She was simply dealing with a problem that had been thrust upon her.

''In a minute.'' He was grateful she didn't say anything more. Moments later, the sharp pain in his knee subsided into a throbbing ache. ''Gotta watch those turns." He tried putting weight on his leg, then grimaced.

He heard her soft gasp, then saw recognition on her face. "You used to be Rick Scott, didn't you?"

CHAPTER TWO

SOMETHING FLICKERED in his eyes and a corner of his mouth lifted. "I guess I was."

She was *not* making a good impression on this man. "I meant, you used to play football. You quarterbacked for the Wolves, right?"

He looked away as he tried his leg again. "You mean you just recognized me?"

"Yes." Was he bothered that she hadn't recognized him before?

"Then why did you follow me?"

"You seemed familiar." And like someone with a story.

"I should. We both work for the *Globe*."

"I know that, but I've never seen you there." Just an empty desk beside hers for weeks.

It had been his grimace of pain that had helped her put a name to his face. She'd seen that expression before, splashed across the front of the sports section and replayed from endless camera angles as Rick Scott, quarterback for the Omaha Wolves and former University of Texas star, received his career-ending injury.

The Wolves had been bound for the playoffs when Rick dropped back to pass and, seeing none of his receivers open, ran with the ball. He nearly made it to the sideline and a first down before he was tackled in front of a nest of photographers.

But that had been several years ago. Ivy watched as he massaged the muscles around his knee. "Does it give you much trouble?"

"You mean other than the fact that I can't play pro ball anymore?" He straightened, testing his leg.

Ivy straightened, too. "Do you miss playing pro ball?"

"Only at times like these." He started walking away. Slowly.

She'd been dismissed. Again. And Ivy had been dismissed one too many times today. She caught up to him. "So you resent female sportswriters, too, is that it?"

He stopped, hands on lean hips. "Not usually."

"Then why won't you talk to me?"

Rick began walking again. Ivy kept pace with him. It was easier now.

"Because I don't want to listen to you whine about discrimination."

Very carefully Ivy asked, "Does that mean you think I might be entitled to a little whining?"

A look of horror passed over his face. Ivy knew exactly what he was thinking: that she was a militant feminist ready to file suit. "Hey, back there—" he jerked his thumb in the general direction of the Colts' locker room, "—that's just guy stuff, you know? And a lot of women *like* to be noticed by men. They expect—"

"Men are such egotists!" Ivy gripped her notebook so hard it crackled.

"With good reason," he shot back.

Ivy glared. "And *football* players are the most egotistical of all!"

Rick raised an eyebrow. "Bad day?" There was that half smile again.

"Couldn't you tell?"

"I don't know—some women enjoy locker-room visits." Amusement flashed in his caramel brown eyes. Intelligent eyes. Mocking eyes. "I know I would."

Ivy clenched her teeth. "Fortunately, women's sports are much more civilized. The athletes actually show up in the interview rooms. Men won't. That's why female reporters were forced to demand access to locker rooms."

"Lot of good it did you. It's a good thing I came by."

"What were you doing there, anyway? This was *my* assignment."

Rick shrugged and walked on. "Talking to old friends." His pace quickened.

Ivy followed him as he hobbled down the wheelchair ramp into the blessedly cool concrete shadow of the stadium entrance tunnel. "Were you spying on me?"

"You sure are paranoid." His voice reverberated in the graffiti-coated walls.

"Well, were you?" They emerged from the tunnel into the heat-softened asphalt parking lot.

Rick whipped around to face her. "Yes. Okay?" He cupped his hands around his mouth and shouted, "I was spying on the *Globe*'s new woman reporter!" Faint echoes sounded in the tunnel they'd just left. He dropped his hands. "I just wanted to see you in action. So sue me."

Ivy narrowed her eyes. "I might."

Rick made a disgusted gesture and limped off.

"Where are you going?"

"To my car."

Ivy scanned the deserted lot. A few school buses were all she could see. "Where's your car?"

"On the other side." Rick didn't seem concerned.

Ivy was, though. Earlier his face had paled with pain. Now he was preparing to hike around the stadium. "What about your knee?"

"You're determined to pry out all the gory details, aren't you?"

"I was asking out of the natural concern one human being has for another."

"You're asking because you're a nosy female," he muttered, stopping to massage his knee.

"I heard that!"

"I'm not surprised."

Ivy maintained a dignified silence as the August sun scorched the top of her head. Heat waves shimmered up from the asphalt. She'd learned that people often filled conversational silences, saying the first thing they thought of, sometimes telling her more than they would have in response to a direct question.

Silence made people uncomfortable.

"Look," Rick said, straightening, "I had some scar tissue removed this summer. That's why you haven't seen me around. My knee still isn't a hundred percent and sometimes when I put weight on it the wrong way, it hurts. I can walk okay, but side-to-side movement gives me trouble." He grinned disarmingly. "Sorry about giving you a rough time."

Ivy responded to the grin, eager to forgive him. "No problem. Pain makes people grouchy." She hesitated, then offered, "If you wait here, I'll go to my car and drive back to pick you up. That way you won't have to walk around to the other side of the stadium."

Rick looked down at her with an expression that said he'd prefer to refuse but was thinking better of it. "Okay."

Ivy ran in the oppressive heat to the other parking lot. She half expected Rick to use the opportunity to escape, then consoled herself with the thought that he couldn't go anywhere very quickly.

A few minutes later, she drove her small Geo around the edge of the stadium. At first she couldn't see him, but as she approached the wheelchair ramp, he emerged from the shadows.

He folded his lanky frame into the little car. "I see you're another Texas grad who didn't want to leave Austin." He nodded to the burnt-orange Texas Exes decal displayed on the rear windshield.

"Yeah, but I'm lucky. I found a job."

Rick chuckled. "Such as it is. Most people use the *Globe* as a stepping stone to fame and glory. You're the third reporter I've had to break in." He glanced at her. "So, where are you headed?"

"I just got the job." Ivy gazed at him. Where was *he* headed?

"When did you graduate?"

Ivy suspected Rick really wanted to know if she'd attended the university when he'd been the Longhorn quarterback. "This past May," she told him. "But I started late. I would have been a freshman the year you took the Longhorns to the Cotton Bowl."

"Yeah." He stared into space. "That was some year."

She heard the wistfulness in his voice.

"You were great," she assured him impulsively.

"Were." He pointed to a Jeep near the few remaining cars in the north parking lot. "That's it."

Ivy pulled up beside the modest vehicle. Not the type of car usually associated with quarterbacks. Even ex-quarterbacks. Nor was it the type of car associated with family men. Ivy noted his ringless fingers as he gripped the dashboard.

"Thanks, and listen," Rick began, hesitating before continuing, "you seem like a nice girl...."

Ivy wanted to throw up. *A nice girl.* She was twenty-four years old and the most *adult* man she'd seen all day was telling her he thought she was a nice girl.

Well, she was nice. Occasionally, she'd tried being not nice, but nobody was fooled.

Not even herself.

"...pick sports reporting?"

Ivy hadn't been paying attention, but she could guess that Rick had asked her why she'd chosen to be a sports reporter. "I love sports. I can write. They seemed to go together."

He stared at her. "Locker rooms aren't nice," he commented finally.

"I know."

"You can't be nice in them."

"But I can be decent and professional."

He opened his mouth, then shut it and looked away. Ivy could see the muscles in his jaw working.

When he was ready to speak again, he obviously picked his words with great care. "You have to be aggressive and thick-skinned. Persistent and annoying. Come to think of it, you're already pretty annoying."

Ivy swallowed and felt tears. Why couldn't she outgrow this habit of bursting into tears? She hated it. She could hardly ever win arguments, because all her energy went into suppressing her tears instead of thinking of a calm and logical response. She certainly couldn't allow herself to cry now. She couldn't even appear to be struggling to hold back tears. It would be disastrous. She blinked rapidly and held her breath.

"See?" Rick snapped his fingers and pointed at her. "You're too sensitive for this job."

Great. He'd noticed. Ivy released her breath. "It's just been a long day and I'm tired."

"Too bad!" Rick's expression was unsympathetic. "You've still got a deadline to make. This is a high-pressure job, and if you want to keep it, you'll have to toughen up."

The tears weren't going to fall. "Thanks for the advice."

"That wasn't advice, but this is—don't write a 'look how nasty the Colts were to little ole me' piece. No player will talk to you if you do."

Ivy scowled at him. "I wouldn't have written that! Give me credit for some intelligence."

"Sweetie—" She glared. Rick immediately held both hands up, palms out. "Sorry, sorry. Ms. Hall—"

"Ivy is just fine."

He nodded. "I know you aren't stupid and I also know you came away pretty light on facts. Sonny Collin was my high school coach. Let me help you out."

"Why?" Ivy shut off the ignition and turned to face him.

"Because."

Ivy raised an eyebrow.

Rick raised his eyebrow right back. "Because I'm a nice guy?"

"You just lectured me on how being nice wasn't an asset."

Rick bit the inside of his cheek and the corners of his eyes crinkled. "How about because you're so cute?"

Ivy gave him her don't-mess-with-me glare again. It did not seem to have an effect.

Rick laughed. "Hey, lighten up."

Of course he was only testing her sense of humor, and Ivy didn't mind that. What she minded was being called cute. Competent, professional, *respected* sportswriters weren't cute.

But she laughed to show him she had a sense of humor. To show him she could be one of the guys, if given a chance. "Really, though, would you help me if I were a male reporter?"

To his credit, Rick considered her words before replying. "I see your point. You want to be treated like everyone else, right?"

He sounded as if he'd heard that before, but Ivy nodded anyway.

"You're not going to have the same problems that a man has, but you *are* going to have the same problems any new reporter would have."

"I know that. I just don't want to be patronized."

"Sure," Rick agreed. "I'll admit I do feel a little sorry for you—can't help it—but on the other hand, I'm still on vacation. I don't have a deadline. You do. The college issue hits the stands on Saturday morning. That means you'd better turn in something by tomorrow night, right?"

Ivy nodded. Actually, her editor had asked for her article by tomorrow morning—Friday. Fourteen hours and ticking.

Rick leaned back, extending his long legs as much as he could. "Besides, after this, you'll owe me. If you were a guy, I'd offer you the same deal."

They stared at each other and Ivy grinned. "Now *that* sounds more like it." She flipped open her notebook. "Okay, Rick, whatcha got?"

Confident Colts Predict Easy Win Over UT
by Ivy Hall

Her first sports byline with the *Globe*. Ivy smoothed the special college-football issue over her desk and smiled into the telephone receiver. "Are you sure you can get more copies?" asked her oldest sister, Holly.

"Yes," Ivy assured her, laughing. "What are you going to do with them all?"

"I'm sending fifty to Laurel and Jack so they can casually display them in their agency's reception area."

Ivy rolled her eyes at the thought of her glamorous sister displaying the *Austin Globe*'s college issue in the equally glamorous Hartman Agency in Hollywood.

She continued to admire her article as Holly outlined the rest of her distribution plans. There was nothing like seeing your byline in print. Staff reports weren't the same. Ivy inhaled deeply, enjoying the sense of satisfaction that stole over her.

The story, laced with some of the cleaner locker-room quotes guaranteed to inflame any Longhorn player who read them, focused on Colts quarterback Taylor Brown and his quest for fame and glory at the expense of the Longhorn defense.

Ivy reveled in the power of the press.

"And I think it's just as good as any of those stories they put on the cover," Holly declared.

A little air leaked from Ivy's bubble of happiness. "The cover usually goes to the senior writers," she explained, trying very hard to keep all traces of defensiveness out of her voice.

"Well, you're on your way!" her sister said bracingly.

She knew Holly meant to be encouraging, but sometimes her sister was a little *too* encouraging. By the end of the call, Ivy had no doubt she was expected to be as spectacularly successful as her sisters.

She was even a bit depressed by the time Billie stopped by to drop off film.

"Nice work, Hall." Billie cocked a hip against her desk. "Coach Collin had a lot to say to you."

Ivy shrugged. "Quite honestly, anything of value he said to Rick Scott."

"Ricky's back?" Billie glanced around the newsroom.

"Not officially." Ivy glanced around, too. Had Rick seen her article? What did he think? She hadn't relied all that much on his information. In fact, she could have written the article without it, but including his comments had added depth.

"Heard about your interview with Taylor Brown." Billie snickered and leaned across her desk. "Was the locker room everything you thought it would be?"

"And less." Ivy pulled the newspaper out from under Billie's hip.

"There she is—the *Globe's* newest ace reporter!" Rick flashed Ivy a grin and collapsed into the chair behind the adjacent desk.

That grin tugged at something in Ivy, something she wasn't quite sure she wanted tugged right now.

"Welcome back, Ricky." Billie tipped an imaginary hat and scooted off Ivy's desk. "Hot enough for you?"

"Go away, Billie," Rick said.

"When I'm good and ready, Ricky."

Billie remained standing, with her arms crossed over her chest and a smug make-me-leave expression on her face.

"Aw, c'mon, Billie. You don't have to protect her from me. I'm not the enemy."

"You're a man, aren't you?"

"Babycakes here can take care of herself, or haven't you heard?"

Billie snorted. "'Course I heard. Everybody's heard."

"*What?*" Ivy squeaked, ignoring the babycakes crack. She'd get him back some other time. "You didn't tell anyone about... about what happened with Taylor, did you, Rick?"

"Well, maybe a few—"

"Are you kidding?" Billie interrupted. "You're *the* topic in locker rooms everywhere."

"Oh, swell." Ivy groaned.

Rick laced his fingers behind his neck and propped his feet on the desk. "Yes, you're practically a legend. You can thank me later. Or you can thank me now."

Ivy wasn't sure she wanted to thank him at all. "What do you want?" She tried to sound agreeable and not suspicious.

"Oh..." Rick looked at her consideringly. "How about writing the annual high school football statistics piece for me?"

Ivy swallowed. Statistics articles involved a lot of research and a lot of verification. Dry and tedious work. "My byline?"

"You got it," Rick agreed immediately, then dropped his feet to the floor and yanked open a desk drawer. "Here're last year's files." He pulled an armload of folders out of the drawer and heaved them across the aisle.

Ivy's eyes widened at the pile of folders now gracing the top of her desk. "But—"

"Gosh, look at the time." Rick stood and began walking backward. "Great working with you," he called as he turned and made his escape.

Ivy stared at the files. "I think I've been bamboozled."

"I *know* you've been bamboozled." Billie guffawed. "But he's got such a handsome mug no one'll blame you."

Heat seeped into Ivy's cheeks. He *was* handsome and she'd better be careful. Rick had done her a favor, but after this, she thought, gazing at the stack of files, they were even.

Billie slung her cameras over her shoulder. "Gotta go. See you at the game. Remember, a woman has to do twice the job a man does to be considered half as good. Luckily, that's not hard."

Ivy was still chuckling when her editor, Boyd Harris, came over to her desk. "Ivy, I heard about the other day. You handled yourself okay." Mr. Harris looked down at her and absently smoothed his tie. "I'd like to tell you that sort of incident is unusual, but it isn't. I don't think any of the teams at UT will give you a problem, but the out-of-towners and the pros..." He ended his speech with a little shake of his head. "Your story is fine, especially considering the tight deadline, but more general than I prefer in my features. You'll really have to dig in. One of the advantages of putting out a weekly sports newspaper is that we have the time to go into more depth. It's essential that you get along with these people, or you won't land a good interview."

Ivy inhaled slowly. What would her editor have said if she'd written the article without Rick's help? "I understand. This time I had difficulties acquiring printable quotes." She didn't want to complain and she wasn't about to tattle on the coach, but thought it only fair to keep her editor informed. Ignoring the problem wouldn't solve it.

Mr. Harris's watery blue eyes regarded her sternly. "You did ask for the assignment."

"I know, and I'm asking for one on the game this afternoon."

"Sure," the editor answered immediately.

Ivy brightened. He trusted her! Now she could show Rick what she could do without his help.

"Rick'll be there, too."

Ivy slumped. Sure, she could cover the game. With Rick there, her editor knew he'd have a good story.

Mr. Harris's hoarse chuckle told her he'd seen her disappointment. "You can solo in time. I will say this about your piece—I'd hate to be Taylor Brown when the Longhorn defense reads those comments."

"Thanks." Ivy was pleased, though she tried to hide it.

"Let me give you some advice." Mr. Harris perched on the corner of her desk, a popular spot, she realized. "Don't try to compete with Rick. He knows a lot of players and coaches. And, of course, he's had game experience. I hired you because I thought you could add to my newspaper. Although I'm not supposed to notice, you *are* female. Try a different slant, concentrate on the players." He slid off the desk. "By the way, now that we've got the college issue out, it's time to put together one on the high schools. I'd like you to write the statistics piece this year. Rick usually does, but he hates writing it, and this will familiarize you with the teams." Mr. Harris knocked twice on her wooden desk and left.

She'd been given the statistics assignment? A smile stole over her face. Rick had tried to collect on the favor she owed him a little too soon. Served him right.

Rick Scott.

Ivy stared at the file folders he'd left on her desk and tapped her pen. There wasn't enough time before this afternoon's game to start researching. The newsroom was clearing out as the remaining half a dozen reporters and photographers left for their assignments.

Rick Scott. He was an intriguing, attractive man, but the pain that she'd seen on his face the other day haunted her. The end of a dream. The end of a career. How did he feel about it, really? And what had happened?

Ivy decided to pay a trip to the morgue, or rather, the newspaper's editorial reference department—one of the first things she'd learned was that the term "morgue" wasn't used anymore. There was a clipping file on Rick Scott, as there was on every major figure in the news. Seven or eight years ago, Rick Scott had been big news in Austin.

Ivy riffled through the clippings, pulling several photographs out. There it was again—the close-up of Rick's grimacing face as he lay on the sidelines, helmet off.

And there were a couple of "Poor Rick" stories, stories rehashing his injury-plagued career. He'd been drafted by the San Antonio Tigers and had sustained his first injury during training camp. He'd missed the rest of that camp and a chance at becoming a starter.

Two years later, he'd been traded to the Wolves. Another injury. Nearly every clipping Ivy found seemed to discuss Rick's injuries or his recovery from them, whether he could play or whether it was too soon for him to play when he did. His pro career, such as it had been, was over by the time he was twenty-five. The announcement of his retirement, dated three years ago, was the last clipping in his file.

Ivy was saddened. He'd been a superstar at the University of Texas. The best in a huge state that lionized its football heroes. And now he was the senior sportswriter for a midsize weekly sports newspaper. Not even a national newspaper.

Rick had every right to be bitter. She would have been. But at least his sports career had left him some valuable contacts. Contacts she didn't have and for which there was no substitute.

Her stomach rumbled and she glanced at her watch, noting with surprise that she'd spent more than an hour reading Rick's file. She was late.

Luckily, both her small one-bedroom apartment and the *Globe* office were within walking distance of Memorial Stadium. Streams of people, dressed in burnt orange and white, were already heading across the sprawling University of Texas campus by the time Ivy got there. She joined them, her press pass saving her a wait in line.

She pushed her way to the crowded press box, searching for Rick.

He stood off to one side, apparently waiting to be interviewed by a local television station.

A man with moussed hair and bronzed face beckoned to him. Rick eased himself into a chair and turned his aw-shucks grin toward the camera. Thirty seconds later, he'd given a concise analysis of this year's Longhorn team versus the team he'd once led to the Cotton Bowl.

He wasn't camera shy at all, Ivy noticed. So why hadn't he chosen to become a sports commentator? He was bright and articulate and certainly had the right looks. Cheekbones like his photographed well. His hair was thick, with no sign of thinning at his crown or fore-head. No shoe polish on the scalp to fool the camera.

Overall, Ivy was impressed.

He finally saw her. "Ivy!" He gestured for her to fol-low him. "You're late."

"Am I?" she asked, trying not to seem defensive. "The game hasn't started yet."

"Ivy, Ivy, Ivy." He shook his head. "What am I go-ing to do with you? I wanted to introduce you to some people."

Ivy could have kicked herself. If she hadn't been pok-ing into his file, she would've arrived much earlier. "I'm sorry."

"No problem. Stick with me and I'll introduce you to the Longhorns later. It'll be easier if I'm with you the first couple of times."

Rick's offer was tempting, but it was important to Ivy that she succeed on her own.

But wasn't writing the story also important? Shouldn't she use every advantage available to her? Rick had con-tacts, but she knew Rick. He was *her* contact. When she thought of his offer in that light, she was grateful.

She tilted her head. "Why are you doing this for me?"

Rick grinned. "'Cause you're a nice girl."

Nice. There was that word again. Ivy didn't want to be nice.

She knew what happened to nice girls.

CHAPTER THREE

NICE GIRLS ENDED UP covering little kids' soccer.

The next Longhorn game was out of state, and Rick got the assignment. Ivy had been sent to report on the start of the Austin Youth Sports Association girls' soccer season.

Soccer. *Girls'* soccer. What a waste of good football-reporting time.

Normally, Ivy would have shrugged off the assignment as paying her dues, but she'd stopped by her apartment to make a sandwich before going to the field. Naturally, she'd checked her answering machine and naturally, it had blinked at her. She suspected it was a Holly blink and she was right.

Holly had wanted to know what Ivy would be writing about this week and was there any chance she'd be coming to Dallas? Ivy hadn't had the heart to call Holly back and tell her she was covering elementary girl's soccer and not college football.

But that was only Holly's first message. The second was to inform Ivy that Laurel and Jack were coming to Texas on business and was there any hope of a sisterly reunion in Dallas?

Ivy hadn't returned that call, either.

The third message was from Laurel, asking whether there was any hope of Ivy, the future Lois Lane, coming to Dallas.

At which point, Ivy had grabbed her sandwich and left.

She parked her little teal-colored Geo in a junior high school parking lot, unwrapped the tunafish sandwich and popped the top on a can of diet soda. It wasn't that she didn't want to see her sisters, it was just that they made her feel so inadequate. She loved them and they meant well, but...

Holly, the oldest, was the owner of Deck the Halls, a Christmas decorating service. And she was obsessively driven. She would have made an excellent man, except that now she was Adam's wife and the super mother of two-year-old Nicholas.

Laurel, the middle sister, had womanhood sewn up. Gorgeous, self-confident Laurel was the epitome of glamorous womanhood. She and her husband, Jack, ran their own talent agency in California. The Hartman Agency was wildly successful, largely due to Laurel's outrageous act of getting married in a red wedding gown. The resulting publicity had drawn hundreds of inquiries, and when Laurel and Jack had returned from their honeymoon, they immediately assembled a full client list.

Ivy would never dream of attracting such attention. She was the shy one in a family of overachievers.

She fanned her face, uncomfortable in the hot car. Soccer practice was due to start at five-thirty and she was early. Maybe she should talk to the coaches, a few parents and a player or two so she wouldn't have to stay for the entire practice. Even if she had to stay, at least it was Wednesday. A slow news day.

She saw a couple of boys' T-ball teams practicing on the other end of the large playground. Three kids toting trombone cases and books straggled out of the band hall to climb into one of the minivans lined up in the circular drive. When Ivy was in school, she, too, had played in the band, but she'd chosen flute. Flutes were small and easy to carry. Since Ivy had no musical calling, that had seemed as good a reason as any for choosing an instrument.

She munched her sandwich and glanced at her watch. Five twenty-five and not a soccer player in sight.

Had she come to the right school? Although this was a junior high, the elementary teams practiced here. Ivy was checking her notes just as another of the ubiquitous minivans parked and disgorged two girls wearing shorts and shin guards, one mother with a stroller and another lugging a cooler.

Ivy rewrapped the last of her sandwich, grabbed her can of soda and followed them.

Five-thirty came and went.

By five-forty, two more girls had been dropped off by their parents.

In the next fifteen minutes, more mothers arrived with coolers, folding chairs, strollers, siblings and potential soccer players.

Apparently the girls had been instructed to bring their own balls. They raced over the field or dribbled them in the parking lot, but that was the extent of the practice.

Who was in charge here?

"I'm Betty Kay," a woman with a clipboard announced. "I'm the team mother. Let's go ahead and assign the drink schedule."

Nothing newsworthy there.

"Please fill out these medical forms and print the name you want on your child's shirt. Letters are twenty-five cents each. I'm collecting the money tonight so the shirts will be ready in time for our first game."

At six o'clock, a business-suited man arrived with a little girl in tow. "Look, can't we wait until six to start practice? Elaine has choir on Wednesdays."

"You can ask the coach," a mother replied. "So far, you haven't missed anything."

The man checked his watch and so did Ivy. "Where *is* the coach?"

"We don't know."

"Who is our coach, anyway?" he asked.

"There isn't a coach listed on the roster," Betty Kay answered.

Everyone stared at her.

"Don't look at me," she protested. "I'm the team mother. I don't even know how to play soccer. What about you, Bill?"

Everyone stared at the lone male of the group. "Hey," he said, "I had to get off work just to pick up Elaine from choir." Everyone stared at the others. "You mean we don't have a coach?" someone asked.

Betty Kay shrugged. "Apparently not, unless someone volunteers in the next few minutes."

"I'm pregnant," another woman announced unnecessarily. "So I can't. Where's Mary Ellen? Her father coached last year."

There was a silence broken by loud objections from two girls who had stayed near their mothers and were listening to the conversation. "No! Mary Ellen got to play all the time. If her dad coaches, we won't get to play!"

"Mary Ellen played very well," said one of the mothers.

"Sure, that's 'cause she had more practice than us."

"Anyway, she didn't sign up for the team this year," Betty Kay said. "So I doubt her father will coach."

Ivy checked her watch again. Six-eleven. What on earth could she write about? She had to write something and she had to write it soon. Maybe she could nudge things along a bit.

"Hi," she said, approaching the team mother. "I'm Ivy Hall, from the *Austin Globe*."

"You're a reporter! How nice. Which one is your daughter?"

"No." Ivy laughed and explained. "My editor sent me to cover your soccer practice."

There was a stunned silence.

"Oh," said someone finally.

"Maybe you could call the AYSA office and find out what happened to your coach." Ivy looked over Betty's shoulder at the papers stuck in the clipboard. She pointed to the game schedule. "They've scheduled you for games. I can't believe they'd do that if you haven't been assigned a coach."

"I can," Betty said. She tapped the letterhead. "The office closes at five-thirty."

Ivy shook her head, mentally toying with the idea of writing an exposé on the Austin Youth Sports Association.

"There's Diane!" shrieked the two girls. They ran to the edge of the parking lot where a huge Suburban unloaded an entire Brownie troop. In uniform.

Their leader jogged across the field. "Sorry, but could we change practice to Tuesdays?"

"Jeanette has her piano lesson on Tuesday."

The Brownie leader sighed. "Thursday, then?"

Two more mothers shook their heads. "Trudy has gymnastics, Sarah and Ruth Ann have ballet. They'd be too tired for soccer."

"Excuse me," Ivy said. "But it's twenty minutes after six. Your practice was supposed to start at five-thirty. And you still don't have a coach."

Everyone looked at each other again.

"M.J.?"

The Brownie leader threw up her hands in exasperation. "I can't do it all! Give me a break!"

"Shouldn't AYSA provide you with a coach?" Ivy asked.

Betty Kay answered her. "They organize us into teams, provide paperwork and equipment. Parents volunteer to be the coaches."

Ivy looked at the group of women in front of her. Bill glanced at his watch and began edging away. Beyond them, their daughters stood around in little groups. A couple of the girls—the only two with shin guards—kicked a soccer ball.

"When are parents supposed to volunteer?" Ivy asked.

"When we sign up our girls to play," M.J. told her with a look at the others that clearly said, "I'm doing *my* part."

Bill spoke. "I think kids today are involved in too much. Elaine already has choir on Wednesdays. She likes choir. She doesn't need soccer. You don't seem to have another day available for practice, so we'll just pack it in." He called to his daughter.

"Wait a minute," Ivy said. "Essentially, we're all standing around here waiting for someone to volunteer to be the coach?"

"Essentially...yes," agreed Betty.

Ivy stared at Bill and the women. On the far end of the playground the T-ball teams had finished their practice. Boys. If these soccer players had been boys, Ivy would have been willing to bet there would have been several coaches.

Where were the rest of the fathers? With their sons, Ivy supposed. Fathers and sons and sports just naturally went together. But girls needed sports experience, too.

Betty Kay sighed. "I've got to go home and cook dinner. Bill's right—the girls have enough to do this season. Let me return the shirt money and we'll call it a day."

By now, more girls had moved closer to discover what was going on.

"When are we going to start practice?" Trudy asked.

"We couldn't find a coach," her mother answered. "And you're already taking gymnastics...."

Ivy heard the other questions and murmured explanations. She supposed she had enough information for a story of sorts. Lack of parental interest and over-scheduled families.

The girls were disappointed, but most accepted it without too much protest.

And that bothered Ivy. The girls should be more upset. They should be griping and arguing and pleading. In fact, two little girls were pirouetting around the field and clapping their hands. Ivy approached them. "Hi, what are your names?"

"I'm Ruth Ann," said the pretty, dark-haired one. "She's Sarah."

"Didn't you want to play soccer?"

"No!" they shouted in unison.

"Why not?"

"Because it's dirty," said Ruth Ann.

"And ballet isn't," commented Ivy wryly.

"No-o-o!" They giggled. "We get to wear pretty costumes, too," Sarah informed Ivy.

"You wear costumes in soccer. They're uniforms, called football strips."

"This isn't football!" declared Ruth Ann.

"They won't have glitter and sequins," Sarah complained. "And you can't wear a crown."

"Well...well, you might win a trophy."

"Soccer is a boy's game," Ruth Ann said, pirouetting off.

Ivy suddenly felt sick to her stomach. Soccer would have been wonderful for these girls. They were going back to ballet and Brownies, choir and piano. Girl stuff.

Nonaggressive stuff.

Stuff that Ivy had done.

She couldn't stand it. She thought of the Colt locker room, the bonding Billie had described and the aggressiveness Ivy struggled to don when pursuing a story.

These little girls had to learn to be aggressive. Assertive. Bond a little.

Ivy watched the Brownies gather by their leader, who held two fingers up in the air. The rest of the mothers collected folding chairs, coolers and assorted younger children. Her heart pounded. She remembered thinking how it felt being naive and gullible. How naturally assertive and self-confident her sisters were.

These little girls could grow up to be just like Ivy.

Shy, sweet and nice.

Nice. Liked, but not respected.

Rick's face flashed into her mind. He probably liked her, but hardly considered her a professional threat. And her editor still didn't allow her to cover big stories by herself.

Then she thought of Billie. Billie, who in her own way was trying to make it easier for Ivy. In fact, Ivy, as a female sportswriter, was allowed in locker rooms only because some other woman had fought for the right.

It was Ivy's turn to help the next generation of women. Giving them experience in team sports was a small thing, but one they desperately needed—whether they wanted it or not.

"Wait!" she shouted. "I'll coach your team."

"What?" someone asked.

"I said, I'll be the soccer coach. I'm volunteering." She'd worry about conflict of interest later.

Everyone froze, then the Brownies began cheering and jumping up and down, making Ivy feel she'd made the right decision. The adults looked relieved. Ruth Ann and Sarah wailed.

"Oh, thank you!" gushed Betty Kay. "Let me have your phone number." She then filled in the appropriate papers.

"When's the next practice?" Bill asked.

"We'll practice on Mondays, Wednesdays and Fridays," Ivy announced to horrified protests.

"Rules limit practices to two per week," Betty Kay informed her.

"Okay, Mondays and Wednesdays."

The objections began.

"At six o'clock," Ivy continued. "Can everyone make that?"

"But dinner—"

"Six o'clock," Ivy repeated firmly. "I'll be here then. Any questions?"

She held her breath, hoping they wouldn't ask if she'd coached soccer before.

They didn't.

Which was good, because she hadn't coached soccer before.

In fact, Ivy had never touched a soccer ball in her life.

AT SIX O'CLOCK the following Monday, Ivy unloaded a cooler, several fluorescent orange pylons and a stack of books with titles like *How to Play Soccer, FUNdamental Soccer* and *Soccer Strategies*.

Sifting through the books, Ivy had second thoughts about volunteering to coach. In fact, she had so many second thoughts, some qualified as third and fourth thoughts.

Well, she reflected, staring at the group of parents congregated around folding chairs, if anyone more experienced volunteered to coach, she'd be happy to let them. Happy? She'd launch fireworks.

Her editor had been very encouraging, welcoming the opportunity for positive community public relations. Ivy would write eight articles about her coaching experiences and the state of elementary-age sports programs.

It wasn't college or pro football, but she was guaranteed a feature article and her picture with a byline in each regular Monday issue of the *Globe.* The recognition allowed her to silence the little voice inside that said she wasn't really pursuing her goal of being assigned stories about pro or college teams. The series also gave her something positive to tell her sisters.

She wanted to tell Rick, but she hadn't seen Rick. He was again out of town on assignment.

Leaving the how-to titles in her car, Ivy selected books dealing with rules and strategies and carted everything to the edge of the parched playing field. Theoretically, she knew how to play soccer, just the way she knew how to play football. Unfortunately, the only soccer game she'd seen was this past weekend after she'd begged a fellow reporter with a cable-TV hookup to let her watch a match.

Soccer wasn't a bad game at all. Actually, the more familiar she became with it, the more she realized that soccer and a good swift kick were just what these wimpy girls needed to compete with the boys.

Ivy blew her whistle, sending a loud, piercing blast to tingle the eardrums of everyone present. Ivy loved her shiny new whistle. It gave her power. It gave her respect.

It also gave her everyone's attention and now she'd better say something.

She opened her mouth, intending to welcome everyone and set some practice rules, when the size of the crowd stopped her. The number of parents and girls milling around was twice what it had been the week before. "Who are all of you?" she asked, instead of her well-rehearsed speech. "I only have fourteen names on my roster."

Betty Kay sidled over. "Well...you see, this is the red team, and they didn't have a coach, either."

"Red?"

"The color of their shirts," the team mother explained. "I suggested they join our team."

"You did?"

Betty Kay nodded. "You don't mind, do you?"

Of course Ivy minded, but what could she say? And thanks to her whistle, everyone now eavesdropped in rapt silence. "Aren't there rules limiting the number of players on a team? There're only fifteen blanks on the roster sheet."

"You're right," Betty conceded—a little too quickly for Ivy's peace of mind. "So you decide who makes the team." She smiled.

Ivy had fallen neatly into the trap. Outmaneuvered by the team mother. What a great start.

Ivy blew her whistle, gratified when Betty Kay flinched. "All right!" Ivy clapped her hands. "Listen up. Let's huddle, uh, sit over here." She jogged to the center of the playing field, out of earshot of the parents. Twenty-three eight- and nine-year-old girls straggled after her. Womanhood's future. Ivy sighed.

"I want a show of hands. How many of you have played soccer before?"

Two hands went up. Fortunately, they belonged to different girls. Ivy recognized them as the girls who'd worn shin guards at the last practice.

She didn't know whether having an inexperienced team was good or not. On the one hand, only two girls would realize she didn't have any soccer experience. On the other, she had hoped to pick up some basics from the more experienced players.

"Why don't you ask how many of us *want* to play soccer." This came from one of the pouting ballerinas.

Ivy stared at her and felt her resolve strengthen. Someday, this little girl would be grateful to Ivy. Maybe not soon, but someday when Miss Ballerina found out that wearing pretty costumes hadn't prepared her for life in the real world, but team sports had.

Ivy blew her whistle. "Everyone on your feet!" Gesturing to one of the girls wearing shin guards, she asked, "What's your name?"

"Lanie," the girl answered.

"See the shin guards Lanie is wearing?" Ivy pointed to what looked like reinforced knee socks. "By next practice, I want everyone to have a pair of shin guards. Also, please wear shorts and shirts you can move in and get dirty. Leave the fancy stuff at home.''

Babble began immediately. Ivy silenced the girls with a short blast from her whistle. "Time to warm up. Jog around the field three times." Ivy drowned out the groans with her whistle.

She really did love her whistle, which was fortunate, since she had to blow it constantly to encourage the girls to complete the three laps. Warm-up took much longer than she'd planned. These girls were out of shape.

When they'd all made it around the field, either jogging or leaping *grand jetés,* Ivy led them in some brief stretches. The ballerinas excelled at stretching.

So far so good, Ivy thought. Time to practice. "The first rule of soccer is that you can't use your hands. That means we've got to practice dribbling—" Giggles interrupted her. "Not basketball dribbling," she continued, though basketball dribbling obviously hadn't occurred to the girls, "but using your feet to control the ball."

"I'm not dribbling on my feet."

Ivy inhaled deeply and grabbed hold of her patience. She might not have had experience, but she *had* read a lot of books, and was prepared to give it her best shot. The least these girls could do was appreciate her efforts.

She opened a book, reviewed how to dribble and attempted to demonstrate running while kicking with the sides of her feet.

She'd expected it to be harder than it had looked on TV.

She hadn't expected it to be impossible.

The girls tried to mimic her. Ivy wasn't sure that was such a good idea.

"Lanie! Help me set up these pylons." They arranged eight pylons in two lines of four each. Ivy blew her whistle. "Line up and take turns guiding the ball around them." She attempted a crisscross pattern, feeling pleased with herself when she managed to complete it.

Ten minutes later, only half the girls had had a turn. In desperation, Ivy referred to her book and set up a "crab" game, where some girls crawled on the ground like crabs and the others attempted to negotiate the ball past them.

She returned to the pylon group, encouraging them, but when she went back to check on the crab game, she found her crabs sitting, talking and braiding one another's hair.

Feeling rather crabby herself, Ivy gathered her own hair and lifted it off her back. It was hot as only Texas in late August could be. Energy-sapping, thought-sapping hot. She could hardly blame the girls for their lack of enthusiasm. But next Monday was Labor Day, so they wouldn't be able to practice. Their first game was the following Saturday, and she had to field a real soccer team. A well-coached soccer team. A disciplined soccer team.

Ivy sighed. It was hopeless.

CHAPTER FOUR

RICK SLAMMED the door of his Jeep and scanned the school playground for Ivy. He'd found himself thinking about her during his locker-room interviews, and when he'd read on the newsroom assignment board that she was here, he'd impulsively driven out.

She was the least likely reporter he'd ever met. She was bright and eager, but that wasn't enough. Successful reporters needed thick skin, persistence and an aggressive personality that bordered on the obnoxious. They certainly didn't win Ms. Congeniality.

Unless they had contacts or had grown up in the area, as he had. He could afford a more laid-back style. But even he'd learned how to dig when he had to.

Of course, the weekly format of the *Globe* did suit Ivy better than a daily newspaper, with its constant pressure, would. He'd thought Boyd Harris had been nuts to hire her, but the last two reporters he'd hired had been hungry and ambitious. After a few months at the *Globe,* they'd gone off to bigger papers.

Ivy was the type to stay put. Then he could leave.

If he wanted to.

Or he could buy the *Globe* and settle in Austin permanently. If he wanted to. He could move out of his town house and build that dream home on his lot at Lakeway. Many University of Texas graduates spent their entire adult life trying to return to Austin. The pretty city was nestled in the Hill Country, just far enough away from the pretentiousness of Dallas and the mugginess of Houston to feel both cosmopolitan and small-townish.

But he wasn't here to make life decisions. He was here to find Ivy. Where was she? Half a dozen teams representing two sports occupied the field. Rick saw several groups of adults, mostly parents, he assumed, but Ivy wasn't among them. At the sound of a whistle, his attention was drawn to a knot of girls in the center of the playing field. There, ineptly battling a soccer ball, was Ivy.

Rick approached the parents, but no one seemed to recognize him. He relaxed and watched the practice, rather impressed with Ivy. She'd been sent to cover soccer, and there she was, learning right along with the girls. He grinned. She might be a great reporter, after all, especially if he... What on earth were the girls doing now?

Rick squinted into the late-afternoon sun. Six girls were crawling around on the ground. Where was their coach?

A blast from Ivy's whistle answered his question. His jaw sagged with the realization that *Ivy* was in charge. He stared at the parents, but they chatted among themselves and generally ignored what was happening on the field.

Rick counted quickly. There had to be more than twenty girls out there. Way too many. Where were the assistant coaches? Rick searched the entire area, then sighed.

What did she think she was doing? Obviously she thought she was coaching soccer. Maybe the coaches were on a break.

But deep down, Rick knew they weren't. He approached a woman with a clipboard. "Excuse me, is she—" he pointed to Ivy "—the coach?"

The woman smiled and nodded.

"The *only* coach? No assistants?"

"No one else could do it."

"No one?" Rick pointedly looked at the adults sitting in their folding chairs.

The woman straightened her shoulders. "I'm Betty Kay, the team mother. *I'm* already doing a job." She gazed at her clipboard. "What have you volunteered to do?"

"I don't have a kid out there! I just came to watch."

The expression on the team mother's face changed. She edged closer to another woman. "Why?"

"I'm a friend of Ivy's. We work together." Rick fumbled for his identification, then realized his running shorts didn't have pockets. "Look—" he nodded toward Ivy "—she needs help out there. She can't handle that many girls by herself."

"She's doing a great job."

Rick settled his hands at his waist and gazed out at the practice. The parents were unbelievable. Most of them were women with younger children, but still. He shook his head, understanding how Ivy had come to "volunteer," but certain she was out of her depth.

A few more minutes of watching convinced him. He jogged over the dried, cracked playing field toward her, feeling like a reluctant white knight.

"Hɪ."

Ivy whirled around. "Rick?" Her throat convulsed in a dry swallow. She'd just been thinking about him, wondering if he knew how to play soccer and, if he did, would he consider a few private tutoring sessions.

He was dressed very casually. Gray had never looked so good. He wore a cutoff, sleeveless sweatshirt, exposing a few inches of flat stomach, jogging shorts and expensive running shoes. His knee was a network of pink-and-white scars, a road map of his career.

He was every inch an athlete, something Ivy was not. She didn't have the build for it, but Rick certainly did. Except for his knee, he appeared to be an athlete in the peak of condition.

Ivy felt hot and rumpled. "What are you doing here?"

"This is where the assignment board said you were." As he answered her, she watched his gaze roam over the scene, then return to her. "I thought you were writing a story, but this looks serious." He tapped her silver whistle and sent it swaying on its cord.

Ivy stilled the whistle. "Writing a story *is* serious."

"So's coaching."

She heard faint censure in his voice. "How long have you been here?"

"Long enough." His face was stern as he pointed to the book she held. "Tell me that's not a how-to-play-soccer book."

"Don't be silly. This is a strategy book. I left the how-to books in the car."

Rick blinked once, then his sandy brows drew together. "What happened to the real coach?"

She did *not* have to defend herself to him. "There wasn't one until I volunteered. The team was just going to disband. Call the whole thing off. Quit." She threw her hands up.

"I see." He sighed and rubbed a spot in the middle of his forehead.

"I couldn't let that happen. And let me tell you, if these were a bunch of boys, there'd be plenty of coaches. Too many coaches." She paused, warming to her subject, preparing to rip his denial to shreds.

"You're right."

Ivy exhaled in a whoosh, like a punctured balloon. "Well . . . girls need sports, too."

Rick sighed again, slowly moving his hands up to rest on his hips. He studied the ground, digging at a crack with his shoe, then stared at Ivy, chewed on the inside of his cheek and squinted skyward into the powdered blue.

At last his gaze returned to Ivy. "I'll help you coach," he said, then grinned. "But only because you look so cute with that whistle."

It was a sexist remark, but Ivy knew it wouldn't be prudent to point that out to her fairy godfather. Instead, she whispered a silent, fervent thanks and followed him to the practice pylons.

"Let's hustle, ladies!" He curled his lip inward and whistled. The sound wasn't as loud as Ivy's whistle, but just as effective.

Maybe more so. Ivy gave a short blast of her own and couldn't help comparing the two sounds. Hers was shrill, tinny and panicked. A femalelike screech. Rick's whistle was mellower, fuller, confident and experienced.

The call of the male *jockus footballus*.

The girls gravitated toward him instantly. Ivy could see all their little budding hormones bursting into full flower. And, she had to admit, eyeing Rick's flat torso and tanned legs, hers were doing some bursting of their own.

"Ivy!" Rick motioned to her, and she trotted to his side, far more breathless than she should have been. "There are too many girls for one team," he said in an undertone.

"That's because we've got two teams here. The other team couldn't find a coach, either."

"Great." He shook his head. "They can't all be on one team."

"Okay, why don't you choose which girls can stay?"

Rick gave her a look probably twin to the one Ivy had given the team mother earlier. "Let me borrow that thing." He leaned down and, without removing the whistle from around Ivy's neck, blew two sharp blasts. They didn't sound tinny, shrill or panicked.

"Ladies, we need to divide you back into two teams. The, uh . . ."

"Red team," Ivy supplied.

"Red team over here." He waved and moved away.

"Turquoise team with me," Ivy said.

"We've got to think of better names," Rick called.

The teams separated into uneven groups. To equalize them, Ivy sent two of her players over to the other side, then she and Rick met in the center. "What's the schedule?" he asked.

"Monday and Wednesday practices, except next Monday, because it's Labor Day. First game a week from Saturday."

His eyes widened. "Okay." He nodded. "Okay," he repeated more firmly. "We can do this. Yeah!" He clapped his hands. "We're gonna play soccer. A week from Saturday." He sounded like he needed more convincing.

Ivy found twelve girls much easier to handle. Rick suggested they hold joint practices. Ivy suspected this was his way of teaching both her and the girls how to play soccer and was grateful for his tact. It didn't surprise her that he knew how to play soccer. He was a natural athlete.

She could really get to like soccer.

At Wednesday's practice, Ivy cynically noted the increased number of fathers—and brothers—in attendance. She had introduced Rick to the mothers at the end of Monday's practice, and obviously word of the Longhorn legend's participation had spread.

The men appeared confused, Ivy thought. They wanted to discuss football with Rick and apparently forgot the game of the day was soccer. She blew her whistle just as a reminder.

As the girls warmed up, Ivy realized she'd been so grateful he'd volunteered to help she'd never asked Rick why he'd sought her out at Monday's practice. Now, watching him, she felt a qualm at the sight of the surgical scars. Would coaching soccer be bad for his knee?

Rick strode, with no noticeable limp, toward their practice spot, his team, Rick's Rockers, skipping behind. Ivy could see some would-be defectors among the girls of her own team, Ivy's League.

Rick had thought of the name. After considerable grumbling, her team had accepted it, but only because Ivy wouldn't let them call themselves the New Kids on the Block's Greatest Fan Club in the Universe. The fact that the name wouldn't fit on the T-shirts didn't concern the girls.

She could hardly blame them for wanting to be on Rick's team, though. She wanted to be on Rick's team herself.

It didn't even matter what the game was.

"Good practice!" Rick called an hour later. "Remember that Monday is a holiday. Make-up practice on Tuesday."

"Don't forget to review the rules!" Ivy called, referring to the handout she'd prepared for the teams. Papers fluttered as the girls ran back to their families. "They're not going to read the rules, are they?"

"Probably not. Shall we pray for rain next Saturday?" Rick asked.

"Not unless you want to get wet," Ivy replied. "No rain days. The game must go on."

Rick muttered and began stacking pylons.

As she watched him, she thought about what a lifesaver he'd been. It was hard to believe he'd ever been a glamorous pro quarterback. The quarterback part, Ivy could accept, but Rick didn't have the insufferable cockiness that usually went with the part. Briefly she wondered if that had something to do with his shortened career, then decided she wasn't being fair to Rick. She thought of the way he gently organized and encouraged the girls, the way they all looked to him for leadership. Rick was a quiet leader rather than a flamboyant one.

Ivy felt a pang. He would have been one of the great all-time pro quarterbacks if he'd been able to stay healthy.

She imagined interviewing him. He would have treated her with courtesy and respect, as one professional to another. "Have I thanked you for helping out here?" she asked suddenly.

He smiled. "About a million times."

"Well, here's a million and one. I really appreciate it."

Rick's smile widened to a grin and he nudged a soccer ball with his foot, bounced it, then kicked it above his head, spun and caught it.

"Pretty fancy, " Ivy acknowledged. "You've played before."

"Long time ago." He bent down and rubbed his scarred knee. "Gotta watch those turns." He grinned again, minus the jauntiness of before.

Ivy moved away, gathering her own equipment, allowing Rick to salvage his male pride in case he needed to limp or rub his knee some more.

"How about joining me for something cold to drink?" he asked, testing his knee, then walking toward her without any sign of either embarrassment or a limp. "Or dinner, if you haven't already eaten?" He slipped the rest of the question in casually and, to Ivy's ears, platonically.

One of the guys talking to another guy. Ivy's initial reaction was disappointment, and then she was irritated with herself. This was exactly the way she wanted to be treated. Just one of the guys. Right?

Right. Unfortunately, a deadline loomed. "I'd like to, but I'm on deadline. I have to head back to the office." They began walking toward the parking lot.

"The basement has a great selection of vending machines," Rick offered.

Ivy laughed. "You're on." She opened the tiny trunk of her car and dropped in assorted soccer equipment. "Did you know that I'm doing a series of articles on my experiences as a coach?"

"And here I thought you were doing this out of the goodness of your heart."

Ivy launched an immediate protest. "I would have coached those girls even if—"

She broke off as Rick signaled time-out. "I was only giving you a hard time, Hall. Let me load this stuff into my Jeep and I'll follow you over to the paper."

Ivy nodded silently. Hall. Just one of the guys.

Fluorescent lights greened the nearly deserted newsroom as Ivy and Rick reached their desks. Since the *Globe* was a weekly publication, the pace was slower than at a daily. Late nights were usually confined to the weekends, since the paper hit the stands on Mondays.

Rick opened a drawer in his desk and withdrew a paper cup filled with coins. "What can I get for you?"

Ivy had already turned on her computer monitor. "I'd like a diet anything with whatever sandwich appears freshest."

"Be right back." Rick saluted with the cup and ambled toward the vending machines.

He returned to an oblivious Ivy. She was tapping her story into her computer terminal with a single-mindedness he recognized. He didn't want to disturb her, so he opened a can of soda and set it near her left hand. Ivy, never taking her eyes off the screen, reached out, took a sip and continued typing.

As he watched her, Rick thought of the thousands of stories he'd written under the same modest circumstances—after hours, fueled by stale sandwiches, cold coffee or warm sodas. Most people expected something more elaborate, more important. Something resembling the newsrooms of the old black-and-white movies.

He wondered what had drawn Ivy to sportswriting. She was no athlete. She was delicate, petite. Someone who appeared smaller than she was. *Sweet.* The word whispered through his mind. She was too sweet for this business. And it would eat her alive.

Ivy read over what she'd written. Nodding, she punched a button on the keyboard and swiveled in her chair, grabbing for her soda. "Gone. Off to copy editing." She brought the drink to her mouth, then lowered it with a shake. "Empty," she said with a puzzled look. "Have I eaten my sandwich?"

"It's still here." Rick nudged the plastic-encased bundle across her desk.

"Yuck. Now I have to taste it." Ivy peeled away the plastic and bit into the sandwich.

Chuckling, Rick propped his feet on top of his desk. "Tell me how you got into sportswriting."

Ivy took a long time to answer. "I love sports. My dad and I had season tickets to the Dallas Cowboys and the Texas Rangers. I'd memorize statistics and he'd show me off to his friends." She smiled wryly. "There are very few professions where one can use sports stats."

"You know my stats?"

"Six-two, 195, caramel-colored eyes, an aw-shucks grin and a gimpy knee."

Rick gave a surprised laugh. "Those are vital stats."

"You said it," agreed Ivy with a mocking leer.

"So you memorize everyone's vitals?"

"Only the stud muffins."

Rick made a strangled sound. "What brought that on?"

Ivy rolled her eyes and tossed the rest of her sandwich into the trash. "When I tell people I'm a sportswriter, the first thing they comment on is the locker room—as if that's the reason I chose this career. Women never ask about the writing part, all they want to know is how does so-and-so look in the buff." She slid him a sidelong glance. "Men, too. It helps if you strike first."

"*I* wasn't going to attack your career choice."

"Weren't you?"

She examined him with a directness that made him distinctly uncomfortable. Privately he thought she was a little too sensitive. She'd have to toughen up or else be miserable her whole career. He'd started to tell her that when he noticed the sudden expression of astonishment on her face. She was gaping at something behind him.

Rick turned and admired the approach of a striking blonde in a tight red dress.

"Ivy, honey, *there* you are!"

What a knockout. Rick blinked, belatedly registering the fact that the bombshell called Ivy by name.

"Laurel?"

The uncertain tone in Ivy's voice drew Rick's attention. She looked stunned. And not a happy stunned.

"Jack and I called and called. Holly said she has, too."

"I haven't been home to check my messages," Ivy mumbled.

"For a week?"

Ivy shrugged. "I stay busy."

The blonde's gaze swiveled in Rick's direction. He dragged his feet from the desk top to the floor. There was a moment of silence.

"Laurel, this is Rick Scott. He's senior writer for the *Globe*. Rick, this is my sister, Laurel Hartman..."

As Rick stood and reached for the hand Laurel offered, he caught the word "sister." Suddenly Rick knew a whole lot more about Ivy. He sensed her hanging back, waiting for his reaction to the glorious female creature she'd just presented to him.

The glorious female creature seemed to be waiting for homage, too. Rick still held her hand, searching for exactly the right thing to say. Something for Ivy.

"... and my brother-in-law, Jack."

Jack's hand was outstretched, and Rick had to release Laurel's hand to shake her husband's. A husband who managed to appear amused and challenging at the same time.

"Good to meet you both. I've enjoyed working with Ivy. She's very talented." Rick tugged gently on a lock of her hair. "It's not often you find beauty and brains in the same package."

Okay, it was corny. Real corny. And it was just the kind of sexist remark she hated. But when he saw the soft, pleased look enter her eyes and the small smile she hid when she ducked her head, he was glad he'd said it.

Laurel tossed her hair, capturing his gaze again. Rick knew her type always liked to have everyone's attention. "Jack and I are in town for the governor's reception at the capitol."

"Which began twenty minutes ago," her tuxedo-clad husband reminded her.

"That's right. The one to promote the film industry in Texas. Laurel and Jack are talent agents," Ivy explained in an aside to Rick. "I'd heard about the reception, but I guess it didn't occur to me that you'd come in from Los Angeles for it."

"It would have if you'd checked your answering machine."

Ivy wilted right before Rick's eyes.

"Don't blame her," he said, jumping to Ivy's defense. "She's practically lived here for the past couple of weeks. We all have. In addition to our usual issues, the *Globe* puts out two special sports issues. In fact, Ivy's on deadline right now." He hoped Ivy's sister wouldn't make a sarcastic remark about the currently empty newsroom.

Laurel arched a brow, then her husband grasped her shoulders. "We need to leave. You don't want to miss meeting any potential contacts."

Laurel patted his hands, then leaned toward Ivy and kissed the air next to her cheek. "Jack and I are flying to Dallas to see Holly tomorrow. Meet us for breakfast?"

As Ivy and her sister firmed up their plans, Rick shook Jack's hand once more. "Take care of her," Jack murmured with a nod toward Ivy.

"I will," Rick found himself promising, though he had no idea why.

Jack kissed Ivy on her cheek, put an arm around his wife's waist and urged her out of the newsroom.

The room seemed abnormally quiet and still after they'd left.

"So that's your sister," Rick said at last.

"One of them."

The phone on Ivy's desk rang. Rick nearly laughed aloud at her expression of relief as she snatched up the receiver and immediately grabbed some paper.

He watched as she wrote, elbow propped on her desk, a hand impatiently pushing her long hair out of the way.

She wore her brown hair long and straight, not in any of the current short styles. He liked it.

He liked her. She was unpretentious and not dazzled by the fact that he'd been a football star. And she understood sports. She enjoyed sports. Ivy would never gripe about watching Monday Night Football. In fact, she'd probably insist on it. She might not be as flashy as her sister, but that actually made her more appealing to Rick. Flashy women required a lot of maintenance.

Ivy hung up the phone, saw him watching her and smiled.

Rick was entranced. Until that moment, he hadn't realized that Ivy's smiles were rare. This was a lovely, gentle smile, no more than a ripple across a serene surface. "You have a beautiful smile," he told her.

Ivy ducked her head and twirled her pen. "Is that what's known as a quarterback sneak?"

"Maybe a pass."

"Oh." To her extreme annoyance, Ivy blushed. And not just any blush. Her cheeks burned. She knew her face was a bright lobster red. A startling red. An infrared glow-in-the-dark red.

She couldn't accept compliments without blushes and she couldn't accept criticism without tears.

She hated being shy.

Why hadn't she inherited the self-confidence of her sisters? Rick was flirting with her, and yet she didn't know how to respond. Men mostly treated her as a buddy or a little sister and she was comfortable with that.

Until now.

"Thanks," she said finally, feeling inadequate.

Rick gave her a boyish smile that made her breath catch in her throat.

She wanted this man to notice her as a woman. Not as a reporter. Not as one of the guys. As a woman.

There were tricks to getting men to notice you, but Ivy wasn't familiar with the art of flirtation. She had scoffed at Laurel when Laurel expounded on men. Ivy knew plenty of men, but she knew them as sweating, muscled jocks. Pals.

She'd watched her sister in action tonight, just as she'd watched her a hundred times before. She'd noticed the way Laurel had tossed her head, drawing attention to her hair. Laurel had a repertoire of smiles and gestures she used automatically.

Frankly, Ivy had always sneered at her sister, thinking she herself was above all that. Now, seeing Rick's smiling face, she knew it wasn't so. She wanted him to look at her the way he'd looked at Laurel when she'd walked into the newsroom.

"Was that phone call anything I need to know about?"

"No." Ivy shook her head. "Just some information I needed for the statistics piece."

Rick seemed slightly embarrassed. "Sorry to drop that assignment on you." He gestured to the files on her desk. "Need some help?"

"Sure." Since he still didn't know Mr. Harris had assigned *her* the story, Ivy handed him three folders and managed to keep a straight face.

He groaned and flipped on his own monitor. "I made the offer in a weak moment. I should've known you'd take advantage of it."

"Rick?"

He turned to look at her inquiringly.

"Thanks... for the help tonight and with the soccer. And for, uh, well, for the nice things you said about me."

He started to say something, then stopped.

"What were you going to say?"

A devilish half smile revealed a faint dimple. "I was going to tell you that you have the prettiest eyes. Soulful eyes. Deep. But I got away with one sexist remark tonight and I figure a second will get me in trouble."

Ivy blinked. *Think of something to say,* she ordered herself. She opened her mouth. Nothing came to mind. She closed her mouth. She glanced down at her pen.

"Am I in trouble?" he asked.

Shyness held her in a paralyzing grip. "No." Ivy couldn't meet his eyes. She was furious with herself. She was acting like a teenager. A young teenager.

"Hey." His voice was kind and too understanding for her peace of mind. "You're welcome. Glad I could help. Okay?"

Ivy looked up and was lost. Lost in warm brown eyes set above photogenic cheekbones. Lost in the seasoning creases life had etched into his face.

Lost in an unprofessional infatuation with Rick Scott.

CHAPTER FIVE

SHE HAD NO BUSINESS thinking mushy thoughts about Rick Scott. Workplace romances were doomed from the start.

Anyway, Rick probably already had a girlfriend.

Or two.

Besides, Rick got along with everybody. She couldn't believe he was singling her out romantically. He was being friendly. Helpful. If she continued to overreact to a little friendliness, she'd be setting herself up for humiliation and embarrassment.

"Ready to go in, Hall?" Rick gestured at the locker-room door.

Speaking of humiliation and embarrassment. Ivy swallowed so her voice would be clear and firm. Confident. Nonchalant.

"Sure." Her voice sounded squeaky and chirpy.

Rick smiled in sympathy and cuffed her on the shoulder. "You'll be fine."

Ivy appreciated his encouragement, except that she shouldn't need encouragement. She was a professional. She should be over nerves.

She shifted from foot to foot as echoes of the teams' school songs died away. Bugs, attracted by the stadium lights, dive-bombed her. Another football game was over. The University of Texas had beaten a nationally ranked team that'd been expected to beat them. Longhorn fans were jubilant.

She and Rick were going to interview the losers.

Reporters, nearly all male, clogged the locker-room entrance. Rick touched her arm. The trainers were admitting the media. Bodies and cameras pressed against her. Ivy pushed behind Rick, finding it difficult to breathe. Everyone was shouting.

She wanted to scream.

At last, she neared the doorway. Rick slipped inside and another reporter shoved her out of the way. Ivy shoved back and a bar of steel encased in flesh blocked her way.

She was face to chest with a huge man with a thick neck. "No women in the locker room."

Ivy gazed up, way up, at him in astonishment. "What?"

"You can't go in. Coach's orders."

Instantly Ivy knew that once this man had struck fear into the hearts of football players on countless opposing teams. One did not annoy this man.

She straightened, not that the scowling giant would notice the fractional increase in her height. "You have to let me in. It's the law."

The arm remained in her path. "Don't know nothin' about any law. Coach says you can't come in."

"But..."

Around her, the male reporters pushed their way inside. Sneaking in among them was the only other female reporter.

Ivy lunged forward. "I need to talk to the players. It's my right." She fumbled for the laminated plastic hooked on her necklace and waved her press card at him. "I'm a reporter."

The man shook his head. "Wait in the interview room."

"No!" Ivy protested. "The players won't go there. They'll go directly to the team bus. I want to speak with the coaches, too."

As the last of the reporters squeezed inside the locker room, the man shook his head and closed the door.

Ivy couldn't believe what had just happened. How was she supposed to locate the interview room? How was she supposed to get her story? Where was Rick...? No, this wasn't Rick's problem. This was her problem and she had to learn to take care of herself and stop depending on Rick.

Inhaling deeply, she pounded on the metal door with the palm of her hand. "Let me in!" She grabbed the doorknob and twisted.

It was locked.

"Hey! The door's locked! That's against the fire-safety codes!"

No answer.

Ivy dropped her arm and became aware of the curious stares of spectators on their way to the parking lot.

She was attracting attention. Ivy hated being the center of attention. In desperation, she looked around, then sent an agonized glance skyward. Immediately, she spied the press box. The interview room. She could reach the interview room through the press box.

Okay, she'd play by their rules. She wouldn't make a fuss; she would register a calm and thoroughly professional objection with the team's management and their school's chancellor.

That's what she'd do, Ivy decided, as she climbed the hundreds of steps that led to the press box at the top of the stadium. Once there, she maneuvered around the phone banks and proceeded to climb down just as many stairs until she was at ground level once again. But this time, she was inside.

Breathing heavily, Ivy prowled through dimly lit corridors until she found the visiting team's locker-room door. She started to knock, thought better of it and tried the knob.

Unlocked. Finally something was going her way.

Entering, she found herself in what had to be the interview room. It was deserted.

Gray tweed covered floors and furniture. Glass walls allowed her to see stadium offices and another corridor, where signs directed athletes to the showers one way and the parking lot the other.

Ivy pressed her face against the glass, her breath fogging it up. Like a kid in a candy store. She leaned back, positioned one of the chairs so she could see the instant anyone rounded the corner and sat. Then she stood and paced. After several long moments had passed, Ivy marched out of the interview room and toward the showers.

And faced another locked door. She pounded on it and the same man answered.

"So where are the players?" She thrust her chin forward, hoping she looked determined and not to be trifled with.

He jerked a thumb over his shoulder. "Be out in a minute." He started to close the door.

Ivy stuck out her foot.

Her foot got pinched.

She gasped, pulled it back and watched the door shut.

Breathing deeply, she willed the door to open again. Then she limped back to the interview room.

Twenty minutes later, as Ivy was losing her battle with impending tears, a few players, clad in team blazers, straggled out.

She quickly wiped her eyes and flipped open her notebook. The young men glanced at her through the glass walls and kept walking.

Just as she'd expected. They didn't want to be interviewed by yet another reporter. Their team had lost a game it had been expected to win.

She jumped up from the scratchy chair and yanked open the door so hard the glass rattled.

"Ivy Hall with the *Globe!*" she shouted after them.

The football players kept walking until they reached the parking lot where team buses waited, engines idling and stinking up the night with diesel fumes.

Ivy stopped short of following the players onto the bus. Other teammates were already seated.

Teammates who'd exited on the other side of the stadium.

A knot formed in Ivy's stomach. She ran back to the interview room, then passed it and continued to the locker-room entrance. The door opened this time.

The damp, steamy room was almost empty.

A familiar figure looked at his watch and stood at the other entrance, obviously waiting for her.

"Rick." Her voice was choked.

His head snapped around and his brows knit. "Where've you been?"

Ivy walked toward him, gingerly picking her way across the slick floor. "They wouldn't let me in. They told me I had to wait in the interview room, and then not one person came to talk to me!"

"Aw, Ivy." Rick's hands rested on his hips as he shook his head. "The coach is a jerk. He was in a foul mood because this loss will drop his team out of the top ten."

"Oh, gee. Is that supposed to make me feel better?" Ivy flipped her notebook shut.

"Hey, let's hit the Longhorn locker room."

Ivy sighed and nodded her agreement when all she really wanted to do was bury her hot face in Rick's broad shoulder and sob. She almost did when he draped his arm around her back. She'd seen football players do the same thing dozens of times and wondered if it felt as comforting to them as it did to her right now. The heavy weight of Rick's arm made her feel stronger, made her feel like one of the team, the *Austin Globe* team. The two of them together were stronger than they were apart.

Ivy smiled up at him, intending to let him know that she appreciated his friendship, when something in his eyes stopped her.

It was awareness. Awareness of her as a woman and not just as a fellow reporter.

Ivy recognized the expression, not because it had been directed at her so very many times, but because she'd seen it in the faces of innumerable men when they'd encountered Laurel. She'd seen it on *his* face when he'd met Laurel.

Ivy and Rick stared at each other for one of those timeless moments in which everything changes, yet nothing is said.

Rick's lips parted. He looked almost surprised.

Ivy's heart pounded. Rick was thinking of her as something other than a reporter. He was seeing her as a woman. He needed time to get used to the idea.

She needed time to get used to the idea.

Rick smiled now, but his smile was a little frayed around the edges. Casually removing his arm, he cleared his throat. "Ready?"

Be cool, Ivy. "Won't everyone be gone by now?" she asked as they strolled toward the home team's locker room.

"You kidding? They won. They'll hang around telling stories for as long as someone is there to listen."

And they were. The atmosphere was completely different. So was the locker room. It was considerably plusher than the facilities for the visiting teams.

Rick introduced Ivy to so many players and coaches that she didn't have time to see their faces, because she was constantly writing down their names.

Rick never left her side and Ivy managed to relax. He suggested questions, story angles and underrated players who were hungry for attention. Ivy came away with more than enough information.

She was satisfied until she studied her articles in the *Globe*'s next issue. Without Rick, she couldn't have written any articles on college football. This was the second time he'd come to her rescue.

When would she ever be able to get a story on her own?

"FIVE LAPS. Move it!" Ivy barked. She hoped she sounded like an army drill sergeant. She was trying to.

"Coach Ivy," whined several voices.

"Let's hustle, ladies!" Ivy punctuated her commands with blasts from her whistle.

She was impatient with the girls today. Actually, she was angry with herself and was taking it out on her soccer team. Well, the exercise wouldn't hurt them. They needed to toughen up.

Bond.

She had only two and a half months to turn them into a lean, mean, soccer machine.

Okay, maybe she was overdoing it.

Ivy still smarted from the locker-room fiasco of the previous weekend. The coach had been wrong, he'd broken the law, but unless she chose to make a huge issue of the incident—not a good career move at this point—it was history.

Oh, she'd written a story, all right. Several of them.

Every one due to Rick's running interference for her in the locker room. And that's what really bothered her. Even with Rick's help, Ivy continued to feel almost sick with nerves before entering a locker room. And once she went in, her mind would go blank at the slightest confrontation.

When would field reporting become easier? She had to toughen up, had to stop looking like the insecure novice she was.

Had to become more like her sisters.

Ivy blew her whistle, encouraging the slower runners. Being shy made reporting very difficult. If she intended to stay in this career, then she needed to train herself to become more assertive.

"Hey, take it easy," Rick said from behind her. "You want your team to have enough energy left to practice, don't you?"

"Exercise is good for them."

"Exercise, not exhaustion." Rick curled his lip and whistled, then waved his arm, signaling the soccer teams to come to him.

Ivy blew her whistle, just so the girls wouldn't think Rick was running the show by himself.

He cupped his hands around his mouth. "Awright, listen up. How many soccer balls have we got?"

Nearly every girl had brought her own ball. At an earlier session Rick had suggested they buy one so they could practice at home. Ivy was surprised to see that even the ballerinas had followed his advice.

"Great. Okay, four lines." He held up four fingers.

The girls scrambled. Ivy felt a twinge of envy at Rick's easy leadership, but suppressed it as unworthy. These girls were learning invaluable lessons. She didn't want them growing up to be like her, did she?

"Ready? As fast as you can, dribble the ball down field. Okay...go!"

And they went.

"How about some chatter out there?" Rick clapped. "Give your teammates a little support."

The girls cheered. Even the ballerinas.

Ivy sighed. Rick looked down at her. "What's with you today?"

She gestured mutely. "I'm angry with myself, I guess."

"How come?"

"Because of last weekend. Because that other woman reporter got into the locker room and I didn't."

"Don't worry about it." Rick waved away her worries. "She got a lucky break. If that guy had been talking to her, you could've been the one to sneak in."

Ivy had begun shaking her head before he finished speaking. "But I wouldn't have. That's the point. I've never been a pushy person, and you've got to be pushy in this business."

"Are you suggesting I'm pushy?"

He was teasing her, and Ivy didn't feel like being teased. "You don't need to be pushy. You know everyone. Everyone knows you. They're your friends or former coaches or teammates-turned-coaches. I've seen how you operate in the newsroom. You don't call anyone—they call you. I have to dig and dig, while stories come falling out of the sky and land right on top of your computer. And all because you're a man.''

Rick, caught trying to whistle, had to stop while he laughed. "Maybe I work a little harder than that." He curled his lip again, reaching for her whistle when all he could manage was a fizzy hiss. "You're something else, Ivy." He blew two sharp blasts.

Immediately—not when they decided to, but immediately—the teams froze to await his instructions.

These girls idolized Rick. And this time, Ivy admitted that she *was* jealous. They'd even recognized the difference in sound he'd made with her whistle.

"Lines one and three, take a hike to the other side of the field," he shouted. "Dribble toward lines two and four. When you meet them in the middle of the field, pass the ball."

"They'll never understand what you want them to do. They're just kids...." Ivy trailed off as lines one and three raced to the opposite side of the field and re-formed.

They waited. Rick whistled. The new drill began. Flawlessly.

Why did she even bother to show up? Rick had them running on remote control. She continued feeling sorry for herself while soccer balls were dribbled up and down the field.

More than a few girls stumbled and fell. Rick checked his watch. "Let's knock off a few minutes early. They're tired."

"No!" The sharpness in her voice surprised Ivy.

She wasn't the only one who was surprised. "Why not?" Rick asked.

"What do you think will happen in an actual game if you baby them now? They'll collapse. They need to build their stamina."

Rick stared at her, unsmiling. "This is supposed to be fun."

"They can learn something while they're having fun."

"What, exactly, should they be learning, Ivy?"

He knew. She shouldn't have to tell him. Or maybe he didn't know. Boys were treated differently than girls. They took boy stuff for granted. Ivy wanted these girls to receive the same treatment as boys, so that when they entered the locker rooms of life they'd never experience the humiliation she'd endured.

She pointed. "If they were boys, would you quit early?"

Rick groaned and let his head fall back. "Is this going to be another discrimination lecture?"

"I have never lectured you on discrimination," Ivy replied with quiet dignity. "I need to learn how to be more assertive and aggressive." She gestured to the teams. "*They* need to learn to be more assertive and aggressive. Team sports work for boys. They can work for girls."

"So you've set yourself up as womanhood's savior."

Ivy wanted to strangle Rick. She shoved her hands into the pockets of her baggy white shorts. "Just coach them the way you would boys."

"Well, you got your way now." Rick poked his arm under her nose. "See? It's seven o'clock. Time to quit. Okay, coach?"

Inside her pockets, Ivy's hands curled into fists. If she'd been alone, she would have kept the practice going another ten minutes. She grabbed her whistle and blew a furious blast.

The sound must have been Rick-like, because the girls stopped and stared at her. She waved them in and began gathering equipment.

She and Rick walked to their cars in strained silence until Rick finally spoke.

"I'll try not to bring my male prejudice to soccer practice." He tossed orange plastic pylons into his Jeep. "But there's too much aggression in kids' sports. I won't tolerate a win-at-all-costs attitude here. Understand?"

Ivy nodded, chastened. Rick looked like a completely different man when he didn't smile. He looked like a man one didn't want to cross. *She* certainly didn't want to cross him. "I just want these girls to experience team spirit or whatever it is that men feel when they play. When I walk into a locker room, I feel like such an outsider."

"The way a man feels when he walks into a beauty parlor?"

Ivy rolled her eyes. "You don't go to beauty parlors!"

"Not more than once."

Ivy slammed the lid of her trunk. "Try to understand!"

Rick climbed into his Jeep and thoughtfully tapped his fingers on the steering wheel. "I want to show you something. Have you got an hour?"

Ivy really didn't, but the thought of spending another hour with him was tempting. "I guess so." It was important not to sound too eager.

"Great." Rick turned the key in the ignition. "I volunteer as a counselor at a place called CAPS—ever heard of it?"

"No." Ivy shook her head.

"Hop in your car and follow me over there. I want you to see where too much aggression in school sports leads."

CHAPTER SIX

IVY DROVE DOWN a pitted street, her enthusiasm dampening as Rick pulled into the gravel driveway of a dilapidated one-story house. She parked her car at the curb and stared at the discreet, tasteful, well-painted sign verifying that this was their destination. The sign was the best-looking architectural element in the neighborhood.

The CAPS building was in a seedy part of town, out of the shadow of both the university and the state capitol. A low-rent district, avoided by even the poorest of students. Not even on the university shuttle line. No orange street signs or Longhorn decals. This was not a place Ivy wanted to be after dark. And it was already dusk.

She'd expected an office in a shopping center or in one of the buildings downtown. Or perhaps near a trendy little Austin café where she and Rick could eat dinner. *Dream on, Ivy.*

And she'd been dreaming a lot since that moment of awareness in the locker room. Part of her wanted to believe Rick's friendly grins were for her alone, except she knew he bestowed them on his team and other co-workers just as liberally.

He'd always cheerfully answered her questions at the *Globe,* in the same way he answered anyone's questions. He was gentle in criticism and generous in praise—

the kind of leader who could inspire people to search within themselves and give a bit extra.

He would've had a spectacular career. And Ivy had thought a great deal about Rick's career after reading his file. He betrayed no traces of bitterness, but surely such a disappointment affected him in some way. Perhaps she was about to find out how.

Rick stood by his Jeep waiting for her. Summoning a smile, she got out of her car.

"Here we are," he said unnecessarily, gesturing to the building and then stuffing his hands into his pockets.

He's nervous, Ivy realized. Easygoing Rick was never nervous. *He cares what I think about this place.* She was touched and pleased. And determined to be enthusiastic.

"CAPS stands for Counseling Athletes about Pro Sports. That pretty much says what we do. Several former pro athletes are available to talk to college kids or even high school kids about life in the pros. And in the off-season, we can sometimes get guys who still play professionally to come and visit."

Rick continued to rattle on. At length. CAPS this and CAPS that. Ivy couldn't believe it. Rick, the cool and confident reporter, was babbling. His nervousness was as endearing as it was unexpected.

"*Somebody* has to tell it like it is in the pros."

Now he was talking in clichés. Ivy was charmed. And intrigued. "Is this a national organization?"

"I wish," Rick said. "We're only local now." Ivy heard a but-I've-got-plans note of determination in his voice.

They approached the house and she noted the weathered wooden exterior. The paint job was in no better or worse condition than those of the houses around it, with the exception of the neon-orange-and-black graffiti screaming on the house next door. Of course, that house boasted Madame Zola, a palm reader.

Ivy climbed two wooden steps and picked her way across a protesting porch. Her smile was as shaky as her footing. Maybe the inside would be better. It had to be better.

It wasn't.

The front door opened into a reception room, similar to the kind found in a doctor's office. Thumbtacked to the walls were two football posters, neither of Rick. Ivy wasn't surprised. Rick was almost unnaturally modest about his college-football career. She surveyed the room, careful not to let her gaze linger on the cracks above the door, the naked light fixture or the hole in the carpet.

The only sound she heard was the banging of a typewriter.

"Hey, Linc's still here." Rick tapped on a frosted-glass partition. "I want you to meet him. Lincoln Thomas, secretary, receptionist and one of the counselors, this is Ivy Hall. She works with me."

"*The* Lincoln Thomas?" Ivy gushed unashamedly. "Running back for the Cougars? Two seasons rushing for a thousand yards?"

"Yes, ma'am."

Ivy stuck her arm through the opening in the window. Lincoln stopped typing long enough to engulf her hand in his huge paw.

"I'll bet you'll be glad when CAPS hires a secretary," she said.

The silence that followed told Ivy she'd blundered.

"No, ma'am," Lincoln said at last. "I'm the secretary. I have five older sisters. Mama told them to learn to type so they'd always have something to fall back on.

By the time I was fifteen, the learn-to-type advice was habit. Good thing, since I never found time to finish school.''

Ivy, with two older sisters herself, was more impressed that Lincoln had survived five sisters than with the fact that he, who had been a pro running back, was now a secretary.

"Rick, check your messages. There's one you ought to take care of right away."

"Okay." Rick gestured at a sofa. "Ivy, wait here. I'll be back in a sec." He strode out of the reception area, leaving Ivy with Lincoln.

"Have a seat," Lincoln said. "I'd show you around, but I know Rick wants to do the honors and I've got typing to finish." He smiled and slid the window partially closed. In moments, the fast clacking resumed.

Ivy tried not to feel abandoned. Gingerly sitting on a brown plaid sofa, she checked the magazines scattered on a low table. Typical sports fare, along with outdated news magazines and a few financial journals.

Obviously someone had made an effort to spruce the place up. The room wasn't filthy, but it did have the look and smell of a house converted to a doctor's office, then abandoned for some time before CAPS had moved in.

White plaster had been globbed over holes and cracks in the patient-soothing pastel blue walls. Gray wreathed the light switches. The carpet was a mosaic of stains the history of which Ivy did not choose to investigate, and the two other chairs were upholstered in a lapsed beige. She shook her head, knowing that Rick, Lincoln and the other counselors were probably used to the shabbiness. Typical men.

But when would Rick have time to redecorate? Between his assignments for the *Globe*, coaching soccer and volunteering here, when did he have time for anything else?

Ivy felt guilty about getting him involved in the soccer. At least the season would be over by Thanksgiving. She resolved to give him plenty of credit when she wrote her soccer articles. And maybe, just maybe, she could return the favor and help him for a change.

A few minutes later, Rick appeared in the doorway and slapped the wooden frame. "How about a tour?"

"Lead on." Ivy accepted the hand he offered, feeling the strength, enjoying his touch.

Rick opened the door that led to the back part of the converted house and lowered his voice. "Linc says we've got two sessions in progress. We'll have to be quiet."

Ivy nodded and followed him. "Who are you counseling?"

"A couple of guys who were cut from the UT football team because they didn't make their grades during summer school. We arranged for tutoring."

And probably paid for it, too, Ivy decided as she took the grand tour. The rest of the CAPS office was decorated in the same abandoned-doctor's-office style. The Spartan conference rooms held card tables and folding chairs. Ivy could see where medical instruments had once hung on the walls and then been removed, leaving two-tone blue gouges and holes.

Rick quietly opened doors and let Ivy observe a few minutes of the counseling sessions. In one, a student struggled with math. In the other, a student and his counselor, another ex-athlete, pored over the UT course catalog.

"That's Mark Butler," Rick whispered as he shut the door. "He was on his way to the pros but got cut during training camp. No other team ever picked him up. I talked him into going back to school. Now he works here, too.''

Ivy scanned the lists of facts and statistics in her mind, but she didn't remember the name. At least Mark Butler had the good sense to return to school. At least he could afford to do so without his athletic scholarship.

They continued through the rest of the building, with Rick commenting on the backgrounds of the counselors. Ivy noted that most, like Rick, had abbreviated pro careers. It made her realize that once athletes, even famous ones, stopped playing their sport, they dropped from the public's consciousness. She began to wonder about various people and what they were doing now. A feature on former athletes and their present occupations might interest her editor.

The kitchen and dining room of the house had been converted into a snack bar. "Want something to drink?" Rick asked, peering into the refrigerator.

Ivy nodded, accepting a canned drink. She and Rick sat at one of the plastic tables. He pulled out a chair and propped his leg on it, absently massaging his knee as he tilted back his head and drained half the can.

He looked tired and with the deadline for the *Globe*'s next issue in three days, he had little chance to rest.

"How do you find time to volunteer?" Ivy heard the gushy admiration in her voice and cringed. It sounded so fake.

"I make time. Especially for this." Rick sighed and stared off into the distance. "Most of the guys we see here couldn't make it in the pros. They don't have a job and they don't have the skills to get one because they either dropped out of school or didn't learn what they needed to while they were there. They all thought they were going to be sports legends." His thumb traced patterns in the condensation on his soda can. "They're all victims of a winning-is-everything mentality."

"At least they aren't victims of a nice-girls-aren't-pushy mentality."

"Were you?"

"In a way," she answered slowly. "My sisters and I were raised with the idea that there were very definite roles for girls and boys. Holly, my oldest sister, didn't pay any attention. Laurel reveled in her role." Ivy shrugged. "I was Daddy's little girl."

"And yet you chose sportswriting."

"Yes." She wanted to change the subject. "Did you think you were going to be a sports legend?"

"Sure," Rick admitted without a trace of embarrassment. "You have to believe in yourself. It's called self-confidence. If *you* don't believe you can do something, why should anyone else?" His brown eyes gazed guilelessly into hers.

"You're talking about me, aren't you?"

A corner of his mouth lifted. "If the cleats fit..."

Ivy looked away.

"Hey." When she didn't look at him, Rick reached across the table and touched her chin with his finger. "I'm—"

"Don't apologize." Ivy glared. "I am well aware of my personal weaknesses. But I can learn and I will." She saw amused approval in his eyes and gave a wry smile. "It's the mistakes I make along the way I'm worried about."

Rick laughed. "I wish there'd been a CAPS organization for me when I entered the pros. Could've prevented a few of my own mistakes."

"I read about when you injured your knee," Ivy confessed.

"Yeah. One minute I was on top of the world. I had it all, and then, poof." He snapped his fingers. "Everything was gone." Rick spoke in a flat, unemotional voice that told Ivy the memories still hurt. "It was my own fault. My choice."

"You didn't choose to become injured!" Ivy protested.

"No, but I shouldn't have played that day. My knee wasn't healed." Ivy glanced down at his leg where it rested on the chair. The pink-and-white scars looked angry. "I shouldn't have run with the ball—even healthy. It was stupid."

"Then why did you?"

Rick was silent for a long time before answering. "We were trying to win and winning was everything." He leaned forward on his elbows. "I brought you here to show you what happens when kids get caught up in the frenzy of winning. And we, the press, are partly responsible."

"Now wait a minute—"

"We are, Ivy! Winners are made into gods and losers are publicly flogged. We influence public opinion without considering that athletes are human beings."

He cares, she thought. *He really cares about people.*

A wave of affection and genuine admiration washed over Ivy and with it came the longing to touch Rick, a longing so strong it shook her.

Ivy had never desired a man physically the way she desired Rick at this moment. Radiating sincerity, he sat across the tacky table from her, his hair gilded by the evening sunlight drizzling in from the dingy window behind him. She wanted to run her fingers through the unruly layers.

He wore a knit shirt that outlined impressively muscled shoulders, and she wanted to run her fingers over them, too.

She sat on her hands. "And you're worried that I'll teach my soccer team that winning is everything."

"Just take it easy, okay?"

"Okay," Ivy agreed. "If you'll promise not to take it *too* easy with them."

"Deal," Rick said, and held out his hand.

Ivy grasped it, ready for a quick handshake.

But not ready for a jolt that charged clear to her elbow. His hand was warm, callused, strong.

She didn't want to let go. And didn't.

She was caught in his gaze, knowing her eyes revealed her growing feelings for him, knowing she was powerless to prevent it. Rick's grin slipped away, though his lips remained parted.

Ivy couldn't bring enough air into her lungs. Her chest felt constricted, as if she'd been running laps with her team. Her hand began to tremble and, horrified, she jerked it out of his grasp. She couldn't let him know how she felt.

"So, when did you begin volunteering at CAPS?" she asked, desperately hoping to distract him.

Rick blinked. "About a year after I announced my retirement. One of my old high school coaches here in Austin asked me to come and talk to the seniors and their parents. He told me about CAPS." Rick shrugged. "I signed up."

"Who funds CAPS?" Ivy felt safer hiding behind questions.

"Donations." Rick bent and retied his shoelace.

"*You* do a lot of donating, don't you?"

Rick straightened and winced. "It's not a big deal."

Ivy suspected it was a very big deal.

"Anyway, I'm kind of on the board of directors," he offered, not meeting her eyes.

"Kind of?"

"You sound like you're interviewing me."

Rick was on the defensive. Ivy breathed easier. "It's so intriguing to see you sit there and fidget. Naturally, I wonder why."

Rick rolled his eyes and lifted a shoulder. "They thought I might...well, you know, because of...the football thing that, well, that kids might come here if they saw my name." The last was mumbled.

"Eloquently put."

"It didn't work." Rick looked down at his hands. The tips of his ears turned pink. "We aren't exactly overwhelmed with clients."

Ivy wanted to hug him. He was obviously proud of being on the CAPS board of directors and was trying not to show it. She debated whether or not to tease him and decided not to. He was such an easy target. "I think CAPS is lucky to have you on their board of directors."

"Thanks." Rick drained the last drops of his soda, then held the can like a football and threw it into the recycling bin.

"And maybe more people don't come here because they haven't heard of it. If I were a football player and I saw your name connected with CAPS, I'd come here."

"You don't count. You're just dazzled by my charming personality."

"Actually, I'm dazzled by how cute you look in those darling little running shorts." Well, he started it.

Rick stared intently at his thumbnail. "Aw, you're trying to make me blush."

Ivy grinned. "And I almost did, too."

Rick made some inaudible comment, then laughed. "I keep forgetting girls are both sugar *and* spice. You'll do, Hall. You'll do."

Now it was Ivy's turn to blush. Idly she wondered if she could suppress it. She tried holding her breath. No luck.

Rick didn't seem to notice. "You know, I can't figure it out. Our services are free. There's a lot of interest when one of us gives a speech, but once the athlete comes here, we rarely see him again. Or her." He turned a puzzled expression toward Ivy. "We usually tell them to stay in school. Maybe that's it. I guess getting an education isn't popular." He exhaled. "I wish I knew what to do."

Ivy shifted on the vinyl chair. Cracks in its surface scraped her skin. "I've been trying to think of a way to say this without sounding shallow or snobby, but have you considered fixing this place up a little? Redecorating?"

"Redecorating costs money," Rick said immediately.

Ivy imagined she heard faint censure in his voice. "Isn't there a budget for maintenance?"

"Maintenance is one thing, but using grant money and donations for furniture and curtains is something else!"

She'd hit a sore spot. Ivy took a deep breath. "If people come here once and never again, maybe you need to invest in a new image."

Rick was silent, looking around the room, then at her, a challenge in his eyes. "CAPS doesn't have money to throw away on an overpriced interior decorator."

"You don't need a decorator," she said, thinking he did.

"You're right. I've got tables and chairs and a sofa in the reception area." He saw her wince. "So they don't match. People don't come here to see the furniture."

She was bound to insult him sooner or later. Probably sooner. "But, Rick, they look like rejects from a men's dorm."

He smiled tightly. "I wanted the guys to feel at home."

Desperately Ivy searched for something to say. Rick was no longer smiling. She sensed his withdrawal. "Don't you offer counseling to female athletes?"

"Sure, if any would come here."

"Don't you want them to feel at home, too? What about the athletes' parents?"

Rick stood, regarding her warily.

Careful, Ivy. "I know you wouldn't race out and buy gold-plated bathroom fixtures and Waterford crystal. But—" Inspiration struck. "When you played pro football, did your team have a uniform?"

"Yes," he admitted cautiously.

"Everybody on the team wore the same uniform?"

"Yes," he said, obviously uncertain what point Ivy was trying to make.

"Why?"

"That's how you tell the good guys from the bad guys."

Ivy shrugged. "Why didn't you all just wear the same color? You know, if your team color is purple, everybody wears something purple."

"It wouldn't look very professional."

"Oh." Ivy nodded as if considering his answer. "Looking professional is important. Did it improve your playing?"

"No...well, kind of. I mean, we were all members of the same team and the uniform emphasized that."

"But the uniform wasn't strictly necessary for you to play football."

"I guess not."

"What would've happened if you all wanted to save money—for a good cause—and showed up for a game dressed in your practice gear?"

Rick laughed. "Nobody'd take us seriously. Appearances are important—" He broke off as Ivy's point hit home. "Boy, did I walk straight into that trap." He shook his head. "You're telling me the place looks pretty bad, right?"

"Dreadful."

Rick heaved a sigh, wandered to the window and stared out. Wind chimes, belonging to his palm-reading neighbor, clinked in the breeze, audible over the hum of the air-conditioning unit.

"Do you think it makes that much of a difference?" he asked, and Ivy knew he wanted her to say it didn't.

But she had to be honest. "During recruiting season, talented athletes are wined and dined. Coaches and agents tell them about the money they can make, the cars and plush homes they can buy. A lot of them grew up in neighborhoods just like this one, in houses just like this one. *This* is what they want to leave."

Rick came back to the table, turned around a chair and straddled it, slumping over the back. "I thought people would listen to what we had to say and not care where we said it."

Ivy hated to dampen his enthusiasm. "Rick, we're talking about a few gallons of paint, for starters. That would improve this place a hundred percent. That and ripping out the rug in your reception area.'' She didn't mention the couch. Nothing could help that couch. She'd suggest burning it later.

He sat up. ''Paint? No flowered wallpaper?''

Ivy smiled. ''A nice stripe, maybe. Flowers cost extra.''

''Figures.'' He slumped again.

''Look, we can paint the place ourselves. I'll help.''

''You will?''

Ivy nodded. ''I owe you for coming to my rescue with the soccer.''

Rick dismissed it. ''You don't owe me anything. I enjoy coaching.''

''Still—'' Ivy smiled ''—if there's money left over, I'll help you decorate. Believe me, I know how to pinch pennies.''

Rick gazed around the room once more, then at her, his slow smile making her pulse race. ''You're really terrific, you know?''

Ivy felt herself turning pink with pleasure just as Rick reached over the chair back, placed his hands on either side of her head and kissed her exuberantly.

He'd caught her by surprise, and before she could register the fact that Rick was kissing her, let alone kiss him back, he'd released her and bounded out of the chair.

''Linc!'' he bellowed. ''Open up petty cash. I'm going to buy paint! Come on, Ivy. I want you to choose colors. Let's do this right.''

But Ivy's body was registering the kiss. Her lips tingled, her knees shook. Her breath quickened. Her heart pounded. The kiss had been too brief. Not exactly passion flaring out of control, but it sure beat a punch on the arm any day.

She stared after Rick as he strode down the hall, ready to follow him as soon as her legs began to function again. There was paint to be bought, colors to be chosen, couches to be burned, and—Ivy hoped—lips to be kissed.

CHAPTER SEVEN

BUT THERE WAS no further kissing that night, or any other day or night that week.

Ivy was confused, then disappointed, then told herself she should be relieved that Rick seemed to have forgotten all about his impulsive kiss. He treated her in the same casual, friendly way he treated everyone else.

Today was Saturday. Ivy's soccer team had just played and won their first game. Still wearing her coach's shirt, she had raced over to the *Globe,* ready to lay her victory at Rick's feet.

She found them, encased in state-of-the-art running shoes, resting atop his desk as he talked on the telephone. Ivy slid into her seat and flipped on her computer monitor. Time to write this week's installment of Ivy's League. How nice to write about a win after two issues detailing her practices.

She typed the title.

Rick was still on the phone. He acknowledged her presence with the briefest of nods. He hadn't changed out of his red ''Rick's Rockers'' shirt, and a grass-stained soccer ball sat on top of a stack of papers in his file basket. He'd come directly from his game, as well.

She typed her lead. Dull, flat writing.

She deleted the sentence and typed another.

Too cutesy.

She deleted that one, too, and glanced at Rick to see if he'd noticed.

He'd propped the telephone against his ear with his shoulder and was scribbling notes, obviously not giving her a thought.

Ivy let her gaze linger. Specifically, she let it linger on his legs. The scars on his knees were the only blemishes on his perfect athlete's legs. A golden honey color, they stretched out from one of the apparently infinite number of running shorts he possessed and wore during the hot weather. Black shorts, white shorts and all colors in between. Cotton, fleece and a shiny satiny material that highlighted the perfectly toned muscles underneath.

Fortunately, the weather in Texas remained warm for months.

Unfortunately, this did nothing for Ivy's peace of mind.

At last Rick got off the phone. "How did it go this morning?"

"We won!" She beamed, waiting for his words of approval.

"Great." He dropped his feet to the floor and adjusted the angle of his monitor.

Ivy waited. "Did your team win?"

"Hmm?" Rick had already begun typing. He stopped, let his head drop back and thought. "I think the other team scored more goals. But the girls had a blast." He continued typing.

Ivy started to offer sympathy, but Rick didn't appear to be in the mood for conversation. His team had lost. Of course he felt down.

Now she felt down, too. She typed another so-so lead to her story, then stopped. This was ridiculous. Absurd.

Thinking about Rick, obsessing about Rick, was affecting her work and her life. Her sleep.

Other than the fact that they both worked for the same employer, there was no reason they couldn't have a relationship. Rick was unattached. As was she. Office romances were merely unwise, not impossible. So what was her problem?

The problem was that she was waiting for him to make the first move. And why? To avoid the possible embarrassment of not having her feelings returned.

But wasn't Rick chancing the same sort of rejection? Ivy knew she'd be open to extracurricular activities, but Rick didn't because she'd concealed her feelings. Ivy was trying to become more assertive, wasn't she? Well?

The new-and-improved Ivy cleared her throat. "I'm available for furniture hunting this afternoon. How about you? Do we have a budget yet?"

"Furniture?" Rick looked up with a distracted expression.

"September sales, now in progress," Ivy prompted.

"Yeah, sure." He stood and stretched, walking across the aisle to read over her shoulder. "Might want to pep up that opening. Reads a little flat."

Ivy gritted her teeth. "I'll work on it."

"When you're finished, we'll hit a couple furniture stores."

"Such enthusiasm."

"Sorry." He tried to smile, but couldn't hold it. "We lost two counselors last week. There wasn't enough for them to do."

So that was it. Ivy felt a pang of sympathy. "Rick, you didn't mention it." Ivy, the new assertive Ivy, took a deep breath. "I've been thinking that you need publicity. I want to write a feature about you and Lincoln and CAPS. Maybe a series.''

"The *Globe* wouldn't publish it. I know. I write for them.''

"So do I, but they're letting me write about the soccer. Mr. Harris is very supportive of the staff's community involvement. Let me pitch the idea to him.''

Rick looked skeptical.

"Is he even aware that you volunteer at CAPS?''

"Don't know.'' Rick shrugged and smiled, doing a better job this time. "Why not? Go for it, kid.'' He ruffled her hair. "Now rewrite that lead.''

Ivy tucked a long lock of hair behind her ear, wondering if she should smooth the back. She tried to imagine what Laurel would do in the same circumstances, but knew that Laurel hadn't had her hair ruffled since she was a little girl.

If then.

The new Ivy was not faring well.

IVY SUPPOSED it was unrealistic to hope that paint fumes could be an aphrodisiac.

She looked longingly at Rick, who stood on a ladder as he carefully painted around the doorframe on the opposite side of the CAPS reception area. He wore overalls without a shirt, and she could clearly see his muscles flexing as he wielded the brush. Wonderful muscles attached to equally wonderful shoulders supporting the handsome head of an exasperatingly single-minded man.

And paint was the single thing on his mind. It had been for the past five days.

Just wait until her CAPS article was published. Mr. Harris had been enthusiastic, as she had known he would be. Rick would have more clients than he could handle.

She outlined a small heart with her roller and turned to see if he noticed. No, and she would have been embarrassed if he had. Sighing, Ivy dipped her roller into the tray and felt her ponytail slide over her shoulder. She grabbed at it, to prevent it from landing in the tasteful creamy white paint they'd selected for the CAPS building. Unfortunately, she had paint on her fingers and now paint in her hair.

Maybe if she *were* paint, she'd get Rick's attention.

Ivy wasn't much on flirting because she'd never needed to do it. She had more male friends than she had women friends. She was more at ease around men than she was around women. In fact, she knew a lot about men. They confided in her, included her in their outings. Treated her like one of them and, occasionally, asked her out on dates.

But neither she nor her dates were ever comfortable proceeding beyond the "just friends" stage. Ivy hadn't really minded until she met Rick. Rick had been different from the very beginning. She wanted more than friendship with Rick.

In fact, right now, she wanted him to kiss her, but she wasn't quite sure what to do if he did, other than kiss him back. The new assertive Ivy had a lot to learn.

"Hey, Ivy, quit fooling around. If we hurry, we can finish this room before soccer practice."

"Sure, Rick!" She injected a bit too much enthusiasm into her voice, drawing a questioning glance from him. She smiled sweetly.

Actually, painting was not as much fun as she'd expected. It was boring and repetitive. Rick complained about her leaving streaks and missing places. She'd visualized them companionably attacking large vistas of innocuous blue, replacing it with a cream that exactly matched one of the colors in the Oriental rug, which would be the decorative focal point of the room.

They'd ripped up the old carpet and discovered a lovely, or what would be lovely after they spent a few hundred hours polishing it, hardwood floor. Ivy hoped Lincoln would see the muscular benefits of extended buffing and take a break from his incessant typing.

Yes, Ivy congratulated herself, she'd done a spectacular job on Saturday when she and Rick had shopped for furniture. After helping him choose a good-quality reproduction of an Oriental rug, Ivy gently pointed out that the brown plaid sofa did not show the rug to its best advantage, but the claret leather couch in the showroom display did.

After that, Rick offered no resistance to buying deep blue chairs, which echoed the blues in the rug. Nor did Ivy encounter any opposition to her suggestion of a ficus tree and a couple of scheffleras in brass planters. They'd even had money left over. It seemed that Rick's main objection to redecorating had been a fear of ornate fussiness. When they finished painting, CAPS would have a classy reception room that was neither too masculine nor too feminine.

Provided Ivy didn't force-feed Rick his brush the next time he pointed out a spot she missed. Glancing over her shoulder, she painted around a light switch without removing the cover first.

Ivy sighed. After all the hours she'd spent scraping, filling, peeling, prepping and painting, she'd hoped for a thank-you dinner at a restaurant in which the words "quick," "krispy" and "burger" did not appear in the name. A romantic little place with dark corners and

discreet waiters, flickering candles and pristine table-
cloths. A neutral playing field where she and Rick could
meet as man and woman.

She heard a metallic clatter from the other side of the
room. "I think we'd better start cleaning up," Rick said,
climbing down the ladder. "Time for soccer practice."
He smiled at her, blinked and continued to stare.

What did he see? Had he finally noticed her as a de-
sirable female? Maybe she looked cute in baggy, paint-
spattered clothes.

"Cute" wasn't good professionally and certainly
wasn't in the same league as sultry or irresistible, but it
was a start. She could work with cute.

Rick's grin widened and he dropped the brush near his
paint tray. Ivy lowered her roller and smiled in return.
He had a very appealing smile. A devastatingly attractive smile.

She heard the plop of a paint drip, but ignored it. Rick
was looking at her with an unreadable expression in his
eyes. He walked toward her, slowly, deliberately. As if he
were a jungle animal stalking his mesmerized prey. Her
heart beat against her rib cage.

He stopped, inches from her, wiping his hands on a
rag tucked through a belt loop.

She held her breath. *He's going to kiss me.*

She watched his eyes scan her face; she could feel the
heat of his body. Lincoln's typing became jungle drums
echoing the pounding of her heart. Trees outside the
windows cast lambent shadows across his face, turning
his expression into something primitive. Elemental.

Man.

Woman.

Rick raised his hand.

Ivy closed her eyes and tilted her head. Swaying toward him, she anticipated the touch of his lips as he claimed her the way men had claimed women through all eternity.

The drums increased their savage tempo.

"You have paint in your hair."

Ivy halted in midsway. The drums stopped. She opened her eyes to find Rick studying her ponytail.

He touched it. "Dried, too. You should be more careful."

Ivy had not been careful. And she did not now think careful thoughts. She thought wild thoughts. Savage thoughts. Violent thoughts.

Raising her roller, she painted a white swath down the top of Rick's head. "So should you."

She felt wonderful. Vindicated.

And extremely silly and juvenile. They'd probably be late for soccer practice.

She didn't care. She'd just humiliated herself by preparing for a kiss that hadn't happened. And it hadn't happened because Rick obviously wasn't interested in her that way. Still. In spite of the new assertive Ivy. And if he wasn't interested in her after five days of togetherness, then she'd probably always stay "pal Ivy." He'd earned his white latex racing stripe.

He stared at her, unmoving. A drop of paint cried its way down his cheek. Ivy lifted a finger and wiped the paint tear away, leaving a milky trail behind.

Expression unchanged, Rick held out his hand. Ivy surrendered her roller, fully expecting to resemble a skunk in moments.

Rick blinked and looked down at his hand. Ivy had handed him the paint-laden roller part instead of the handle.

"Oops," she said.

They gazed at each other. Madame Zola's wind chimes tinkled, Lincoln's typing clattered and Rick's hand dripped.

Silently, Ivy offered him her own rag, barely used. Before taking it, he bent and carefully positioned her roller in the paint tray.

"You know..." he began, sounding thoughtful.

Ivy swallowed. She knew. She knew she was about to be told off, verbally clobbered and immediately given a one-way ticket out of Rick's life.

"You know..." he said again, wiping his hands, studying the whitened creases and half-moons under his fingernails, "it occurs to me that there is a whole new dimension to male-female relationships in which the rules are constantly changed. Usually by the female."

Why didn't he just get it over with? Take his revenge. Why torture her with suspense?

Rick continued meticulously cleaning his fingers, apparently ignoring his hair. It had stopped dripping, anyway. "For example, a woman entering a predominately male profession, say sports journalism?" He raised his eyebrows questioningly.

Ivy bit her lip.

"She asks to be treated like a man. But not too much like a man. She is, after all, a woman, but males aren't supposed to notice."

"Rick—"

"But being lustful males, we do notice," he continued, unperturbed. "And our remarks are considered sexist, our overtures, harassment." He tossed the rag aside. "However, woe be unto him who fails to notice when the rules of the game change and lustful overtures are not only in bounds, but expected."

Ivy ducked her head, shriveling with embarrassment. Rick tipped her chin with his now-clean finger, compelling her to meet his eyes. "What happens to those poor men who can't read minds, Ivy?"

"They get paint in their hair," she murmured.

Rick stepped closer, picked up her spotted ponytail and tugged. "And do you know what happens to the woman?"

He didn't sound angry. His eyes crinkled at the corners, but his mouth didn't curve. Ivy tried a smile. A tiny, hopeful, daring smile. "She gets kissed?"

"Only if she agrees the rules have changed." Rick looked down at her in a way he hadn't before, in the way Ivy had hoped he would. "Have they changed, Ivy?" he asked softly.

She was no longer one of the guys. She saw desire, real desire for her as a woman, lighting the caramel-colored eyes. She shivered in response.

One of Rick's hands cradled the back of her head, the other nestled in the small of her back and slowly, but inexorably, urged her toward him. "This will complicate things," he said, tracing warm circles at the base of her spine.

The circles ignited an answering warmth deep within her. Ivy lifted her face. "We'll uncomplicate them later," she said.

His lips met hers lightly, giving her a chance to pull back, asking if she was sure.

She was sure. "Waiting for a penalty flag?"

A corner of his mouth twitched. "Thought I might get called for holding."

Ivy stood on tiptoe and clung to Rick's magnificent shoulders, shoulders powering arms that could rifle a football fifty yards down the field.

"I think I'll get called for roughing the passer." This time, Ivy kissed Rick. She kissed him with all the pent-up yearning caused by weeks of admiring his well-shaped legs, appreciating his patience and kindness with the girls and reveling in the smiles he tossed her way.

She kissed him with love.

Her eyes opened wide. *Love?* When had her feelings changed to love?

When they'd sat at the kitchen table and he'd discussed his lofty dreams for this shabby house? When he'd volunteered to coach soccer in spite of his knee? Or moments ago, when he'd gazed at her with a predatory look in his eyes?

Whenever it was, she was way ahead of him. He'd only just begun to think of her as a woman.

"You taste spicy," Rick breathed against her lips.

Spicy. Ivy liked the sound of that. Spicy, not sweet.

Her fingers kneaded the muscles of his shoulders and neck, slipping under the straps of his overalls and caressing the bronze, satiny skin of his back.

Rick inhaled sharply and drew her even closer, burying his face in the side of her neck. She could feel the prickle of his hair, stiffened by drying latex paint.

She voiced a sigh. "If you don't wash the paint off now, you'll never get it out."

"I'll shave my head," Rick replied, capturing her lips once more.

Now Ivy knew why it was called "falling" in love. She was falling, soaring and floating at the same time. It was opening kickoff, halftime fireworks and a winning touchdown all at once. Just for a moment more, Ivy surrendered to the euphoria of Rick's kiss before pulling back. Not too much, too soon.

"You're planning to shave your head by six o'clock?"

Rick blinked, then closed his eyes, resting his forehead against hers.

"Soccer." He sighed.

"Soccer." She sighed back.

"SOCCER STINKS," declared Ruth Ann. "I'd rather be doing something else."

So would I, Ivy thought, remembering the feel of Rick's arms around her.

"I don't know why I have to come to practice since I hardly get to play," the girl continued.

Privately, with her attitude, Ivy also wondered why Ruth Ann continued to come to practice. But then, thinking of her vow to expose these girls to team sports, she smiled encouragingly. "You'd play more if you'd practice the way Lanie does."

"Lanie's brother helps her. I don't have a brother."

"I don't have a brother, either," Ivy told her, wanting Ruth Ann to see that a brother wasn't necessary for a girl to play sports.

"Everybody on Coach Rick's team gets to play." Ruth Ann's gaze was accusing.

"And they didn't win their game," Ivy pointed out, proud of her team.

Soccer practice had started fifteen minutes ago—without Rick, who was still trying to remove the paint from his hair. Ivy, who had removed the paint from her own hair in minutes, had agreed to drill both teams by herself until he arrived.

It was the least she could do.

And this was an opportunity to toughen up Rick's Rockers. She'd set up a scrimmage, and Ivy's League was creaming them. At this rate, she could send in her second string.

She blew her whistle, signaling the end of the period. "Ruth Ann, why don't you sub for Lanie?"

Ivy made some other substitutions, then approached the Rockers. She'd been watching them and had singled out their best players. She sent in these girls to play the last period, ignoring the complaints of those who thought it was their turn. They pouted and flung themselves to the ground.

Typical female behavior, which Ivy ignored. She blew her whistle again and the game was under way.

A freshly showered Rick arrived just as his team scored a goal. "Awright!" He cupped his mouth and shouted, "Good job!" Under his breath, he asked, "How's it going?"

"Great." Ivy smiled up at him, feeling a shy awkwardness. How was she supposed to act? Greet him with a kiss? Loop her arm around his waist? She'd always scorned the cheerleader types who clung to their football-player boyfriends in public.

Rick nodded, smiled briefly and stuck his hands into the pockets of his shorts.

Okay, she was making too much of a simple kiss. No, not simple. Not for her. But she had to remember that Rick couldn't possibly feel the same way about her as she felt about him. If only he'd give her a sign or something.

IF ONLY SHE'D GIVE HIM a sign or something. How was a guy supposed to know what women were thinking—except that they expected him to know?

The last time he thought he had a situation pegged, he'd gotten a head full of paint. He ran his hand through his still-damp hair and thought about how much trouble could have been avoided if he'd kissed her the first time he'd wanted to.

On the other hand, kissing her in the Colts' locker room wouldn't have been the smartest thing to do.

"Coach Rick?"

Rick gave Ivy an apologetic smile and turned his attention to the girl who'd spoken. "What is it, Trudy?"

"*She* won't let me play." Trudy shot Ivy a venomous glance.

"Maybe it's not your turn."

"It is so! I've only played one quarter. It's my turn to play this quarter, but *she* let Colleen play. And she made her play goalie again."

"It's just a mix-up because I was late. We'll straighten this out." He patted Trudy on the arm and sent her back to join the other girls.

"Actually," Ivy began, "it wasn't a mix-up. We were scrimmaging and your team was getting clobbered. The girls I've got playing now are your best. Colleen should be your goalie for every game. She's blocked three shots so far."

Rick nodded. "She's good, but if she plays goalie all the time, none of the others will have a chance to play that position."

"Then they should practice and earn the spot."

"That's not the point." Rick was irritated with her. He didn't want to be irritated with her. Not after that kiss. When she'd kissed him back, he'd felt the way he did after a particularly hard tackle—winded and dazed. One followed through after kisses like that. One did not argue.

"Wait a minute," she said. "You and your teammates didn't take turns at different positions when you played football in school, did you?"

Rick suspected he was about to walk into another trap. "No, but that wasn't the same."

"Because you were boys?" she asked quickly.

Uh-oh. "Ivy... the whole point of participating in organized sports *at this age,*" he stressed, "is to give the kids a chance to learn the game and experience playing. Both boys and girls."

She tossed her head, sending silky paint-free hair over her shoulder. "Well, why can't they do that *and* experience winning?"

He draped an arm over her shoulders and squeezed. "There are things more important than winning." He pulled her close, hoping to remind her of at least one of those things.

To his surprise, she shrugged off his arm. "You wouldn't say that if they were boys."

Rick carefully examined his treatment of the girls. "I would."

"You've been treating your team the same way you'd treat boys?"

"No."

Her jaw hardened and she started to turn away.

"That would be stupid. Physically, they're different, so I'm emphasizing different tactics. Besides," he pointed out, "my team just scored again. That's two since I got here."

Ivy regarded him unblinkingly. "That makes the score eleven to two."

"Really?" He smiled, unable to help it. "I mean, I'm happy for my girls, but what happened to your team?"

"They've scored the eleven." She looked so smug.

It stung. "Rick's Rockers might not win, but at least everyone gets to play."

"Girls have to accept competition, Rick," she explained in a maddeningly superior voice. "One thing I've learned is that in the real world, where men make the rules, if a woman wants to be taken seriously, she has to think like a man."

He'd watched as Ivy had become more assertive over these past weeks. He'd been proud of her, but she was about to go too far.

"Rick," she was saying, "I think you've been too easy on your team. They aren't fragile. They're not going to break. I think you should treat them just the way you'd treat a boys' soccer team."

Rick frowned. "Didn't you read the Austin Youth Sports creed? Everyone gets a chance to play."

Ivy glared at him. "They all *have* a chance to play. Those who are the best *get* to play. If the others improve, then they can play, too. Why should I punish my best players by forcing them to sit out two quarters? Shouldn't I reward them? If the others really wanted to play, they'd try harder."

"How can they try when they don't play!" Rick's voice was much louder than he'd intended. He lowered it. "Your priorities are skewed."

Ivy shook her head vigorously. "Not at all. Being a member of a winning team is important. That's the way it is in life. Those who are stronger and brighter, those who try harder and longer, are the ones who succeed. It's time girls started learning that."

Rick opened his mouth to tell her she was way off base when he realized pursuing the matter was pointless. She was in no mood to listen to his side.

"Ivy?" She looked at him, cheeks flushed. "Let's not argue."

"But this is serious, Rick. We have a fundamental difference in philosophies here. I was coddled, and I'm having a terrible time outgrowing it."

"I might be making practice a little too easy." He held out his hands when she started to speak. "And you might, just might, be overdoing it a bit."

She closed her mouth, not looking as though she agreed, but grudgingly willing to compromise.

Rick reached out with the intention of wrapping his arm around her waist. Ivy jumped away, looking stiff and apprehensive.

"Relax, Ivy. Call me stuffy, but I've made it a rule never to kiss fellow coaches during soccer practice."

"You better not!" Her face turned even pinker.

Rick laughed, promptly put his arms around her and tugged at her rigid body until she stumbled close to him.

Then he broke his rule.

CHAPTER EIGHT

"RICK AND IVY sittin' in a tree. K-i-s-s-i-n-g. First comes love, then comes marriage, then comes Ivy with a ba-by carriage."

The girls had spotted them and were now giggling and dancing around. A mortified Ivy couldn't bear to face the row of parents. Couldn't face Rick. "I guess that means practice is over."

Rick's reply was lost in the general babble.

Blindly grabbing bright orange pylons, Ivy stuffed them into the dirty canvas equipment bag. She felt more like a third-grader than a twenty-four-year-old professional.

As her cheeks cooled, Ivy realized she was furious. How could Rick kiss her in front of the parents? In front of the girls? What was he thinking?

Maybe she didn't want to know what he was thinking.

She hadn't been in love enough times to feel comfortable with the sensation. Feelings other people took for granted were new to her. Rick had seemed to understand that.

A soccer ball had rolled near the edge of the fenced playground. Ivy walked over to retrieve it, hoping most of the girls and parents would be gone by the time she returned.

They were. Rick was already loading equipment into his Jeep when Ivy dumped her sack on the pavement and silently started packing her team's gear into her trunk.

"You know, Ivy, that—" Rick jerked a thumb toward the playing field "—has never happened to me before, and I don't have the slightest idea what to say to you."

"You don't?" Rick the Cool at a loss for words?

"Nope."

"That's what happens when you break the rules." She slammed the trunk shut and fanned her face. "You might try apologizing."

Rick bounced a soccer ball on the pavement, then shot it into a cloth bag with the rest of the extra balls and shin guards.

"I'm sorry I embarrassed you." He looked very contrite for a fraction of a second. Then his mouth quivered. "But I'm not sorry I kissed you. In fact—" he shaded his eyes and scanned the playing field "—if I can find a soccer team somewhere, I might even kiss you again."

"Don't try, unless you're wearing shin guards."

"Relax." Rick cuffed her on the shoulder, something he did whenever emotions ran high. "It was a joke. I'm smiling—see?" He bared his teeth.

A joke. How could he joke about kissing her? Face burning—the September heat had nothing to do with it—Ivy felt the sting of imminent tears. She *couldn't* do something as stupid as cry! The new Ivy did not cry when she was hurt or angry. Blinking rapidly, she turned her head away.

"Hey." Rick touched her chin and forced her to look at him. Ivy knew her eyes glistened with unshed tears and hated herself for it. "The joke was about finding a soccer team, not about kissing," he said gently. "I don't joke about kissing."

"Neither do I," she whispered, her anger seeping away. The afternoon had been full of intense emotions, and Ivy was tired. She didn't want to be angry with Rick. "I just didn't think you were taking me seriously."

"Oh, I take you seriously, all right."

She watched his gaze drop to her lips and knew he was thinking about kissing her again.

And she wanted him to.

Instead, a corner of his mouth lifted. "You know my schedule is about to get crazy. I've got to cover the San Antonio game this weekend, then four more road games."

He was pulling back. Ivy crossed her arms in front of her and leaned against her car. "Good thing the painting is nearly finished." Her voice sounded brittle.

"I'll miss our painting sessions."

Ivy held herself tautly. "I was never that thrilled about painting," she admitted.

His eyes crinkled in amusement. "It had its moments."

"Not that many."

Rick chuckled. "And there aren't going to be many moments in the next few weeks, either. I'll probably miss a few soccer practices. Can you handle them for me?"

"Sure." Ivy could hear the strain in her voice and knew Rick could hear it, too. Maybe he'd think she was worried about coaching both teams by herself.

"Atta girl," he said, putting an arm around her shoulders. "You're very special to me, Ivy."

Ivy's heart sank. This speech was beginning to sound awfully familiar.

"I don't want to ruin what we have together," he added.

Yes, it was definitely the old let's-not-ruin-a-beautiful-friendship speech. Why did she think this time would be different just because *her* feelings were different?

Ivy felt her heart breaking. He'd guessed her feelings, sensed her growing love.

And didn't love her back.

Rick was trying to let her down gently, because that was the type of man he was. If Ivy was very, very careful, she could emerge from this discussion with both her pride and Rick's friendship intact.

"I want to keep seeing you," Rick said.

Ivy quickly turned away. She couldn't bear to face him and hear what came next.

"I value our..."

He floundered for the right word. "Friendship" was the word he was searching for.

She wasn't going to mention it.

"...friendship."

Drat. Let's get this over with. "And you don't want to do anything to jeopardize it or our working relationship, right?" She looked at him then and smiled—a tight, hard little smile.

"Right." Relief washed over Rick's features. Ivy's stomach churned. "I won't get to see you much outside the office." His expression changed, uncertainty replacing relief. "You do understand, don't you?"

"Sure, I understand." Ivy removed Rick's arm from around her shoulders. "I've heard it before—I've even said it before. So long, it's been great. Or something similar, right?"

"Wrong." Rick captured her face in his hands. "I must be losing my touch," he said in the instant before his lips descended to meet hers.

Ivy had given up all hope of being kissed—or anything else. She felt stunned. Thoroughly stunned. Too stunned to close her eyes. Too stunned to breathe.

But not too stunned to feel.

At first she felt only surprise, then the pressure of his lips on hers sparked a response. She closed her eyes as one by one, her senses began to function again. She felt the warm firmness of Rick's mouth, inhaled the dusty outdoor scent that always clung to him. She made a tiny sighing sound as her tightly coiled emotions unwound.

One of Rick's hands left her cheek, moved around to her nape and then splayed across her back, urging her nearer. She broke the kiss in order to encircle him with her arms, enjoying touching the shoulders she'd admired. Corded muscles flexed as Rick pulled her even closer. "I thought maybe you only wanted to be friends," she said.

"Friendship is important." Rick nipped at her earlobe and trailed kisses down the side of her neck. "But I had something more in mind."

"I thought you were telling me you didn't want to see me anymore!"

"Far from it. But things, for want of a better word, will be slowing down. And—" he searched her face "—that might not be so bad."

His half grin tugged at her middle. Ivy swallowed. She knew her inexperience couldn't be more apparent if she wore a label. He was probably bored with her, no matter how kind he was being. Ivy was irritated with herself. She wished she could call a time-out and phone Laurel for some coaching. When guys sought out Ivy to ask for advice, it was girls like Laurel they wanted advice about.

"I'm trying to tell you that I don't mind taking 'things'—" he smiled at the word "—slowly."

"You don't?" Ivy could hear the hopeful sound in her voice.

"For two people who work in communications, we haven't been communicating at all well," he murmured.

"I think I've got the message now," Ivy replied, lifting her face.

"Let's make sure," Rick said as his lips took hers once more. "Very, very sure."

A FEW MINUTES LATER Rick watched as the taillights on Ivy's car winked out of sight.

She was sweet, which meant she could get hurt.

He only hoped he wouldn't be the one to hurt her.

THE FRONT PAGE. The entire front page. With a color photo. And a sidebar with her byline. More inches of story than anyone else. Lots more.

Ivy sat at her desk and hugged an advance tear sheet of the *Austin Globe* to her chest, heedless of creases and smearing ink. She didn't care. She had several more copies. She'd send those copies to her sisters. To her friends. To distant acquaintances. Now Holly would be truly impressed.

Ivy spun around in her chair. A single yellow rose had been waiting on her desk this morning, but there'd been no note.

Ivy snatched up the rose and inhaled the scent of success. She didn't need a note. The rose had to be from

Rick. Carefully, she placed a copy of the paper with her CAPS article on the edge of his desk.

She'd barely spent any time at all with him in the past couple of weeks. They'd passed each other in the office—Ivy going home when Rick, under deadline, arrived. He'd managed to make the Saturday soccer games, but waving at a distance was extremely unsatisfying. The CAPS office was finished and ready for more clients. Ivy was ready to see Rick.

Today she would. It was a perfectly glorious day. The first cool front of the season had arrived, and the air was clear and dry. The sun sparkled and it finally felt like fall. Football weather. And today, she'd see a lot of football. She and Rick were due to cover two out-of-town Southwest Conference games, then drive back to Austin for a UT home game at night. Together. Ivy could hardly wait.

Thirty minutes later, as Ivy was becoming concerned about making the noon game, Rick ambled to his desk. He dropped a quick kiss on the top of her head and flipped on his computer monitor at the same time. "Ready to go?"

Ivy nodded and refrained from mentioning that she'd been ready for more than an hour and that they should have left fifteen minutes ago.

"Just let me check..." His voice trailed off as he studied his computer screen.

Ivy fidgeted, trying to appear purposefully occupied until he was finished. Finally, she couldn't stand it any longer. "Did you see the article?" She sounded shyly breathless. Not the way she wanted to sound at all.

"Sure did." Rick closed his eyes and stretched his arms above him.

She tapped the pristine copy she'd placed on his desk. "For your scrapbook."

She wasn't going to ask what he thought of the article. She didn't care. She was a professional and the only important opinions were her own and her editor's. Mr. Harris—Boyd, as he insisted she call him—had liked it. Loved it, even. In fact, he'd told her that her strength was in features, not hard reporting. Ivy was both pleased and dismayed. She wanted to avoid being stereotyped at all costs. Too many women were assigned "soft" news stories. She'd have to be even more forceful and persistent today.

Rick's opinion about the article didn't matter. So what if she'd spent three times as long writing the CAPS article as she had any other? So what if she'd done so much preliminary writing that she'd been able to file an exceptionally polished piece?

She'd written it for herself, not for him.

She certainly hadn't written it to show him how good her writing was.

The least he could do was read it.

Ivy straightened the newspaper, positioning it so that Billie's terrific photo was facing him on the off chance he should happen to glance down at it. Maybe he'd skim a few words.

Rick grinned, eyes still closed. "The article on CAPS is—" he paused and Ivy's heart nearly stopped "—fantastic. It's the way I would have written it myself."

He'd read it. He'd liked it. Ivy tried not to smile.

Now the day was perfect.

PERFECTLY HORRIBLE.

Between baseball's World Series, pro basketball preseason games and football, sportswriters were over-worked and short-tempered.

Ivy stood in the locker room of the winning team and shouted questions. She was ignored, shoved and steamed. Then she ran to the losing team's locker room and was ignored, shoved and insulted. The number of reporters milling around had doubled from games earlier in the season. Ivy had to fight them, as well as belligerent football players.

Afterward, she met Rick in the parking lot and told herself she'd try harder at the next game.

The second game, in a different city, had started by the time they'd arrived. Ivy, at the suggestion of her editor, had been following certain players throughout the season and reporting on how they fared each week. Some were being considered for national awards, and some were just promising newcomers.

Two were playing right now. Interviewing both would be tricky, but Ivy had the entire game to give herself a pep talk. The long day wasn't even half over. She was tired and cranky. Even Rick's easy smile seemed forced.

After the game, Ivy mentally tossed a coin and went to interview the losers. The winning team had allowed the reporters in immediately, jubilantly ignoring the ten minutes they customarily kept the media waiting. Thus, about the time Ivy was being admitted to the losing team's locker room, swarms of lucky reporters were running for their second set of interviews.

She found herself just as frustrated as she'd been all season. Why did she have to go through this?

Reporting wasn't getting any easier. Until Rick saw her problem and steered a couple of players her way.

"You from the *Globe?*" asked one.

"Yes, I'm Ivy Hall," she responded, positioning her pen.

"Rick said to come talk to you."

Ivy hesitated, but couldn't afford to let the opportunity slip away. She could phone her featured player later. "Now that you've lost to the Cougars, do you still think you'll make it to a Bowl game?"

As the player answered and she scribbled, Ivy felt depressed. Once again, Rick had come to her rescue.

"Better luck this time?" he asked as they drove back to Austin for their third and last game of the day.

"Yes. Thanks." She had to force the words out. "Rick...I really appreciate your looking out for me, but it's October. You shouldn't have to help me get stories. You *never* should have had to. I need to succeed or fail on my own."

He opened his mouth, then closed it. Ivy knew he'd been about to say that she would've failed long before now.

"All season, I've been telling myself that if I only tried harder, if I could only be more forceful, locker-room trips would become easier."

"And have they?" He didn't take his gaze off the road, but rolled his shoulders.

"No, but that's entirely my problem. So—" Ivy reached over to knead at the kink in Rick's nearest shoulder and also to take the sting out of her words "—promise me you won't send me any more of your buddies to interview. Don't tell people I'm your friend and to be nice to me. Okay?"

Rick glanced at her briefly before turning his gaze back to the highway. He was tight-lipped and Ivy knew she'd angered him.

"Did it occur to you that I might have an interest in your success because it would make *my* job easier?"

"You said something like that once."

"Who do you think picks up the slack when the *Globe*'s a man—figuratively speaking—short? And do you think I want to spend the rest of my life playing nursemaid to cub reporters?"

"I see." She'd certainly been put in her place. "I see," she repeated when the silence between them grew uncomfortable.

Miles passed before either made a stab at conversation. After several stilted exchanges, Ivy preferred the silence.

The first quarter of the Texas game was over by the time Rick had found a parking place and he and Ivy entered the stadium. Ivy, without looking to see if Rick was behind her, climbed the concrete steps to the press box and sat. Rick hadn't followed her.

She crossed and uncrossed her legs. She scanned the bleachers. She inhaled the newly crisp October air, tinged with smoke from the homecoming bonfire, and tried to recapture her enthusiasm for football.

Homecoming. Mums. Rhinestone princesses. It was all there. *This* was why she'd chosen to become a sportswriter. The cheerleaders screamed, the crowd roared, the band played. Ivy waited for the familiar surge of adrenaline to come charging through her veins.

Nothing.

She couldn't enjoy anything as long as Rick was angry with her. When the game was over, Ivy squared her shoulders. She knew she'd been right to ask Rick for no further special treatment.

So why did being right make her feel so miserable?

And her misery continued in the visitors' locker room. If she didn't know better, she might have suspected Rick of sabotaging her interview chances. She cut her time there short and trudged over to the Longhorn locker room. It had been a Longhorn victory, so at least they'd be in a good mood.

Good mood failed to adequately describe the scene as Ivy walked in. The team was in a frenzy of joy. They doused their coach with water, beer and champagne. Two minutes after she'd entered the locker room, Ivy smelled like a brewery. The players could shower. She couldn't.

Rick, his hair damp and his own enthusiasm restored, grabbed her arm and pulled her to one side. "Did you see who's here?" he asked, his voice nearly a whisper.

"Who?"

Rick checked to see if they could be overheard and pulled her farther out of the way. "Rudy Allen, the agent."

Ivy was suitably impressed. Rudy Allen was a barracuda, an agent to the sports stars, or the soon-to-be stars. "Who's he representing?"

"That's what I want you to find out. He won't talk to me—we've tangled a few times—but he doesn't know you. Find out what you can."

Ivy smiled with amused exasperation. Rick wanted her to think he needed her help. He just couldn't stop protecting her. "Rick, I thought we agreed you'd treat me like any other reporter."

"Ivy!" He shook her arm. "I'm not spoon-feeding you a story! Now go grill the guy." He turned her around and pushed her toward the showers.

She'd humor him this last time, but only because he'd done such a good acting job.

So, where was Rudy Allen? Ivy hung back, scanning the crowded room for the agent. She vaguely knew what he looked like, and she certainly knew him by reputation.

Then she saw him. A small, wiry man, wearing Rudy's trademark hat, slipped out the side door. Ivy pirouetted around, intending to exit by the shower entrance and catch him outside. She darted through the training room and plowed into a shirtless player, his arm encased in an ice pack.

The UT quarterback.

Ivy couldn't believe her luck. No one else had interviewed him because he'd been injured late in the game. He was on his way to the therapy room.

"Ivy Hall, with the *Globe*," she shouted, her voice echoing in the corridor.

The quarterback looked startled, but recovered quickly and agreeably answered Ivy's questions.

Finally. Luck was finally with her. She was weak-kneed with relief and could hardly wait to tell Rick. She didn't need his tip. She'd found a story on her own. A good one. He'd be proud of her.

As soon as she finished interviewing the quarterback, she ran out and kept running until she reached the parking lot. Rick paced beside his Jeep. Ivy saw him and waved her notebook.

"Well? What did you find out?" he asked as soon as she was within earshot.

"I interviewed the quarterback! First—and maybe it's an exclusive! Look at all my notes!" Laughing, Ivy tumbled into his arms.

"What about Rudy? Who's he representing?"

"Oh. He left, so I didn't talk with him."

All expression was wiped from Rick's face. He grabbed her shoulders. "You didn't find out anything? Nothing?"

Ivy blinked. "No."

Rick's fingers clenched on her shoulders and the breath hissed between his teeth. He muttered something Ivy didn't hear—and didn't want to—and began running across the parking lot toward the stadium entrance.

"Rick! Your knee!"

He either didn't hear her or he ignored her.

More than half an hour passed, during which time Ivy reached the terrible conclusion that she'd goofed. Rick had depended on her. She, with an excess of pride, had let him down.

At last, she saw him, walking slowly, with just the slightest of limps to make her feel even worse.

He unlocked the Jeep, slamming the door after she climbed in.

He was angry. Furious. Livid.

And it was justified.

She watched as he stalked around the Jeep, jerked open the door and flung himself inside. He ground the ignition and jammed the car into gear, then sat, staring out over the dashboard. Suddenly he slammed his fist against the steering wheel.

Ivy jumped.

"I suppose we can always buy a newspaper to read about Rudy Allen's newest client."

"I'm sorry," Ivy said in a small don't-hurt-me voice.

"Rudy has left. The team has left. The trainers have left."

The lights in the stadium parking lot blinked out. "Even maintenance is leaving."

"I'm sorry," Ivy repeated, calmer now. Okay, she'd made a big mistake. She'd admitted it.

"But wait, maybe I could ask one of *them* for a story."

"I'm sorry," Ivy said once more, not quite as sorry as she had been.

"Sorry? That's all you can say? A huge story breaks right under your nose and all you have to say is you're *sorry?*"

Ivy wasn't sorry at all now. "Doesn't the halo get a little heavy, Rick?"

He glared at her, his face pinkly illuminated by the few remaining halogen emergency lamps. Gunning the engine, he stomped on the accelerator. Tires spun. Gravel flew. Ivy cringed.

"Why? Just tell me why you didn't go after him."

"I thought you were being nice to me again!" Ivy snapped. "You're always giving me tips and sending people to me. Half the time you've already interviewed them. How was I supposed to know this time was different?"

"Because I told you so!" Rick snarled the anguished snarl of a scooped journalist. "I told you Rudy doesn't like me. I knew you could get a better story than I could."

"I understand now." But this fiasco wasn't all her fault. "If you'd treated me like any other reporter from the very beginning, the misunderstanding about Rudy would never have happened."

"If I'd treated you like any other reporter, you wouldn't have lasted this long."

"I'll never know, will I?" Ivy said quickly, trying to beat the quaver in her voice. Deep down she believed Rick was right. She *wouldn't* have been able to make it as a reporter. She hated her lack of self-confidence and knew the only way to trust her abilities was to succeed on her own.

They stopped at a traffic light at a deserted intersection. Ivy knew they were headed back to the *Globe* for damage control.

Rick turned to face her, not driving on, even when the light changed from red to green. "All right. Fine. You want to be treated like any other reporter, then I'll treat you like any other reporter, *Ms*. Hall."

CHAPTER NINE

"YES, I'LL TELL HIM you called."

Ivy hung up the phone and scribbled on a pink message pad. Reaching across the aisle to Rick's deserted desk, she floated the paper across his keyboard, where he was certain to find it.

International Sports had called again. Ivy wondered why the monthly magazine was calling Rick, but it was unlikely she'd ever find out.

Though they'd patched up their professional relationship, Ivy knew Rick was avoiding her, since their personal relationship—if those few glorious weeks could be called a relationship—was in tatters.

He'd vowed to treat her like anyone else, but he hadn't. The other reporters were given easygoing smiles and friendly remarks. Ivy received curt nods and mumbled acknowledgments. He didn't even thaw during soccer practices and finally suggested they meet separately, since six o'clock was no longer convenient for him.

He'd deliberately misunderstood her request. She hadn't been trying to end their personal relationship, but he'd made it very difficult to explain. Each time she'd been brave enough to approach him, his unsmiling face and neutral expression stopped her. His eyes, which she'd seen warm to a molten caramel color had hardened to a plain, unwelcoming brown.

Her small apartment was just as unwelcoming, and Ivy spent longer and longer hours at her computer. Though her volume of work grew, so did her personal misery.

Locker-room forays were terrible, emphasizing how much help Rick had actually given her. On the other hand, her in-depth, one-on-one feature articles had won her some accolades. She could relax during personal interviews; only in crowds did her mind go blank.

The phone on Rick's desk rang again. Ivy snatched it up. Honestly, she'd become his personal secretary!

"Rick Scott, please. This is Sonny Collin with the Colts."

A bittersweet memory of her first professional locker-room visit flickered through Ivy's mind. She'd met Rick there. "Rick's on assignment." A euphemism for the fact that he wasn't at his desk. "This is Ivy Hall. Could I help you?"

"Hey, I remember you. You're that girl reporter, right?"

"Yes," Ivy acknowledged, not sure she wanted to be recognized by Coach Collin. They hadn't parted on the best of terms.

"I didn't need to talk to Rick about anything in particular. Just tell him I called."

As Ivy placed yet another pink slip on a steadily growing pile, she thought about the telephone call. A coach wanting to chat to a reporter about nothing in particular?

Not likely.

She resumed work on her current article, but was unable to concentrate. What could Coach Collin have wanted with Rick? They were old friends, but something in the coach's voice... Ivy reviewed what she knew about the Colts. They weren't members of the Southwest Conference, but had managed to produce two spectacular quarterbacks, one of whom, the senior, had been nominated for an award. The other, a junior, was extremely talented, but underused. The more Ivy thought about the situation, the more her instincts told her to investigate.

Several phone calls later, she banged the phone down in frustration. The Colts weren't talking. Of course, she'd only tried the well-known names. Sighing, she picked up the phone again. Now she'd try the second-string players. In her weeks of interviewing, she'd learned that they, flattered by the attention, often had more interesting things to say than the frequently interviewed players with their recycled opinions. Besides, second-stringers rarely had experience in editing their remarks for the media.

She had better luck with this round of phone calls. Apparently there was resentment and jealousy among the players. Too many thought that Taylor Brown, the senior quarterback, was receiving preferential treatment to enhance his chances of winning an award. The team thought he should pay more attention to them, rather than his personal statistics.

Interesting. Ivy left her name and telephone number and indicated a willingness to listen. She glanced at her watch, then at Rick's empty desk with the pink message slips, which fluttered every time someone walked by.

"Hiya, Hall." Billie heaved her camera-laden bulk onto Rick's desk. "How's it goin'? Fighting the good fight?"

Ivy managed a smile. "Fighting."

"Those locker-room trips any easier?"

Shrugging, Ivy intended to make a flip reply. "No," she heard herself confess, instead. "No, they aren't."

Billie slapped her knees. "Bound to. Anyway, it's fun bothering all the men, isn't it?" She tittered.

Was it? Ivy stared at her hands as she thought of the sneering and heckling. She thought of her attempts to remain professional in the face of that antagonism. "No. I hate it—all of it." Once she'd admitted her feelings aloud, she couldn't stop. "I hate the way I feel waiting to go inside. I hate the nasty remarks and the disgusting language. I hate their attitude toward me." She looked up at Billie. "I don't enjoy fighting."

Billie's eyebrows raised, but she didn't seem surprised. "Honey, you picked the wrong job."

Ivy drew a deep breath. "You may be right." She looked down at her hands again. They were clenched.

There was an uncomfortable silence. Ivy supposed Billie was struggling for an appropriate quote. She apparently couldn't find one. "You're too nice, Ivy. Normal people aren't nice." Billie swiveled on the desk and began reading Rick's message slips.

Nice. There it was again. Well, Ivy had tried to toughen up. Tried to be aggressive. All she'd accomplished was to alienate Rick. And he was the only one who mattered to her.

"*International Sports,* right on schedule." Billie held up one of the messages Ivy had taken.

"What do you mean, 'right on schedule'?" Ivy was glad to change the subject.

"They call Ricky twice a year to let him know they're still interested in him."

"Still? You mean they've offered him a job?"

Billie nodded.

Ivy sat back in her chair. There wasn't a sports reporter anywhere who didn't aspire to write for *International Sports*. Travel. Prestige. Money and respect. The monthly magazine also sponsored a cable-television program and some of their reporters had moved into broadcast news. Ivy had even hoped that one day she might... "He's turned them down?"

"Yep." Billie nodded again.

"Why?" Accepting a position—even a small one— with *International Sports* would boost Rick's career. Wasn't that what he wanted?

"Good question." Billie hopped off the desk. "Why don't you ask him?"

Ivy stared at the photographer as she wandered off. Then she glanced at Rick's desk. He'd told her that the *Globe* was a stepping stone for a lot of journalists. So why wasn't he stepping? Maybe she *would* ask him.

Where was he, anyway? She checked the assignment board and didn't see Rick's name. Maybe he was at the CAPS office. Before she had consciously decided to do so, Ivy had scooped up the pink papers and was driving to CAPS. She was overdue for a dinner break, anyway.

She had no idea what to say to Rick. Besides, he might not even be there. By the time she turned down the potholed street, Ivy began to hope he *wouldn't* be there.

But he was. His Jeep sat in the gravel driveway.

Ivy jumped out of her car before she lost her nerve and ran up the front steps. They'd been repaired.

"Hi, Lincoln!" she called, as she breezed in the front door. "Rick here?"

But Lincoln wasn't typing behind the frosted window—Rick was. Rick, clad in the running shorts and cutoff sweatshirt he still wore even though the weather had cooled.

"Hello, Ivy," he greeted her in a horridly bland, disinterested voice. He continued typing.

Ivy's impulsive burst of courage fizzled. She watched his fingers fly over the keys and frantically cast about for a conversational topic.

"The reception area looks great. The...plants add just the right touch." She made a show of studying the room, ignoring the fact that Rick was ignoring her.

When she turned back to the window he'd stopped typing, resting his hands against the keyboard. He regarded her steadily. And silently.

"Business must be great since my article came out." She tried for an I'm-so-glad-for-you tone that ended up sounding peevish.

"Yes, we've added three counselors." He hesitated, then said, "You know we appreciate all your help." A stiff and formal thank-you.

"Actually," Ivy flung out, "I don't know. We hardly speak anymore, and you've never bothered to invite me over to see the final result."

Rick's face softened slightly. "You don't need an invitation to stop by."

"Are you sure?" Ivy forced herself to meet his eyes.

Several heartbeats passed. The hum of the electric typewriter filled the silence.

"Are you still mad at me about the Rudy Allen story?" she asked at last.

"No." Rick clicked off the typewriter. "Everybody's entitled to a mistake or two."

"Then . . . ?" She gestured mutely.

"Why am I avoiding you?" Rick finished the question she'd been unable to ask. He sighed and buried his fingers in the cropped layers of his hair. "Because I can't stand watching you struggle. Those brown eyes of yours get all big and wounded looking. And then you . . . you disappear into the walls, or something. I don't know.''

''I hang around the broadcasters and eavesdrop on their interviews,'' Ivy mumbled.

He gaped at her. ''You'd rather do that than let me send you some players?''

Ivy nodded.

''That's what I can't understand,'' he said, throwing up his hands. ''You keep banging your head against a wall. And yet, every time I think 'That's it, she's outta here,' you write one of those 3000-word beauties.''

He liked her feature articles. He hadn't been completely ignoring her, after all. Ivy smiled and kept smiling.

THAT SMILE GOT to him. The smile and the eyes. Ivy was a gentle, sensitive person working in a brash, tough profession. To succeed, she'd have to change her personality—the very essence of what made her Ivy. And he'd finally admitted to himself that he couldn't stomach seeing her change herself.

He was already three-quarters of the way in love with the person she was.

It hurt to watch her at work. It hurt that she didn't want his help. If he helped her, she wouldn't have to become the aggressive reporter she was set on becoming. Didn't she know that? Didn't she care?

''I missed you,'' he admitted, causing her smile to widen.

''Me, too,'' she whispered in that husky voice of hers.

Seconds later, Rick had moved around the partition and was holding Ivy in his arms. He inhaled the sweet floral fragrance of her hair and caressed the silky strands.

"Ivy," he said on a sigh, his forehead resting on hers, "I want to make this work."

"Then when we're on the job, you'll have to treat me as just another reporter. If I make a mistake, let me have it."

"Sure." She was actually serious. "Yell at you and then say, 'How about a hamburger?'"

"If you yell at me, you'd better offer a steak, at least."

He chuckled, drawing her close. She nestled against his chest, triggering all sorts of protective feelings—feelings she expected him to squash.

"We'll try your way," he murmured because he could think of no other solution. "But no whining about fairness or asking for special favors."

"I never whine!" she objected.

"See that you don't start." Rick dropped a kiss on her nose, then laced his fingers through hers and led her over to the new couch. The leather surface, cool at first, was soon warmed by their bodies. Madame Zola's wind chimes tinkled incessantly.

Ivy traced the scars on his knee. "I haven't had a chance to ask you how your knee is."

"Good as new." Rick was not thinking about his knee. He was thinking about Ivy. Specifically about kissing her and why he was having a sudden attack of awkwardness. They were alone, the mini-blinds were drawn, there wasn't a soccer team in sight and the sofa was a marvel of modern design. So?

She looked up at him and his heart blipped. Uh-oh. He was in trouble.

One look in those eyes and he knew that Ivy was in love with him. She probably didn't know it yet, or she wouldn't let her feelings show so clearly.

Rick was saddened. Either their professional or their personal relationship was doomed. Sooner or later, Ivy was going to get hurt.

He didn't want to hurt her, he wanted to kiss her. But guys didn't kiss girls who were in love with them unless they loved them back—or might love them back. Fun and games were fine as long as both parties knew the rules.

Ivy wasn't a party girl. Kissing her right now would be serious business.

He reached out, his hand skimming the side of her neck. He could feel her pulse fluttering.

Ivy was the best thing to come into his life in a long time. He . . . needed her.

He bent his head, taking her lips with his. He was gentle; she was enchanting, with echoes of remembered passion and the promise of more.

His heart hammering, Rick pulled back. He felt different—as if he'd been blindsided by a 240-pound linebacker.

When he became aware of Ivy's insistent pressing at the nape of his neck, he recognized the breathless feeling.

It was love. He'd fallen all the way in love with Ivy.

Yes, he was definitely in trouble.

And he didn't mind in the least.

"I'M VERY GLAD you dropped by tonight." It was the latest in a string of nonsense that had been the sum of their conversation during the last hour.

"I forgot!" Ivy sat straight up and dug in her jeans pockets. "I actually did have a reason—your messages." She handed the crumpled pink wad to Rick.

He kept one arm curled around her as he sifted through the papers. "Hmm." He rapidly discarded all but two.

"Wait. What about Coach Collin's call?" Ivy retrieved the message slip.

"He just wants me to pick Taylor for the Pros' Choice football team." He shrugged. "I might, I might not."

Ivy remembered the dissension among the Colt players. "Are you sure? He might have some other story to discuss."

Rick shook his head. "I doubt it."

That meant she'd discovered a story all on her own! Ivy hugged the knowledge to herself. This could be her first real break.

The message from *International Sports* was the next to end up in the discard pile. "Hey!" Ivy snatched it back. "Billie told me they offered you a job."

"Billie should stick to exposing film."

"Did they offer you a job?"

Rick glanced down at her, then away as he replied, "They've made job-offer noises."

"Billie also said you'd turned them down."

"See if I give *her* any more tips."

Ivy laid a hand on his arm. "Why? Most reporters dream of writing for *International Sports*."

Rick nodded slowly. "I'd have to move to New York."

"Oh" was all Ivy could manage. Move from Austin? Away from her? She thought of the reporters who'd left before her.

"But I'm not particularly interested until there's a reliable reporter to take my place here."

And she was supposed to be that reliable reporter.

Great. If she became a successful sportswriter, Rick would leave the *Globe*. Leave her.

And if she failed, she'd keep him from a dream job. He'd resent her so much that their deepening relationship probably couldn't survive.

Either way, she realized, her happiness fading, she'd lose him.

A GLORIOUSLY CLEAR and sharp November day signaled the end of the soccer season. The last game, and it was Ivy's League against Rick's Rockers. They were playing for real this time.

Ivy tried not to think of the coming confrontation as anything other than a regular game, but it loomed in her mind as Rick's philosophy against hers. Man against woman.

Her team was undefeated, a fact in which she took great pride. Three girls had quit and Ivy was sorry to lose them. Those who remained had learned the rewards of hard work. Ivy hoped they'd carry the lessons with them as they grew up.

She herself had learned the lessons right along with her team. She'd spent the past week pursuing the Colts story, determined to be the first reporter to write about it. She was also determined to succeed, so if Rick wanted to take the *International Sports* job, her ineptitude wouldn't hold him back.

She wished she'd never heard of *International Sports*. She wished she knew Rick's plans.

And if she was a part of them.

Slamming her car door, Ivy stared out at the field. Way off in the distance, she could see a group of red-shirted girls and a tall man. Rick's Rockers. And Rick.

How could she bear it if he moved to New York?

She'd deal with that when—and if—she needed to.

Goose bumps pricked her flesh as she trudged across the field. Sharp wind whipped her hair across her mouth, bringing tears to her eyes. Yes, that was it. The wind.

His team was already running warm-up drills. Several of her girls had joined in. She waved the rest of them over.

Rick first caught the movement, then recognized her, waved and jogged across the stubbled field. He wore running shorts, still, and a hooded sweatshirt with pockets, into which he'd thrust his fists. "I'm not going to kiss you," he announced, "even though I want to." He grinned and she mustered a return grin.

"Nervous about the game?" He waggled his eyebrows.

Rick must have sensed that something was bothering her. She'd let him think it was the game. "A little."

"Liar—you're undefeated."

"The girls have been great."

"I wanted to talk to you about that. I noticed during drills that your players are either very good at a position, or they act as if they've rarely played it. Some of them told me they don't play any more than one quarter."

"Every girl who shows up gets some playing time." She'd made sure of that after Rick's earlier comments.

He gave her a knowing look. "But only late in the fourth quarter when you're winning, right?"

"Well—" Ivy shrugged "—we usually are winning in the fourth quarter."

Rick checked his watch, causing Ivy to involuntarily check hers, as well. Time for the teams to clear the field. She blew her whistle at the same time Rick curled his lip and let loose with his own blast. His was still louder.

"Why don't you mix your positions and let the girls play where they want today?" he suggested.

"So your team can win?" Ivy shot back.

"Believe it or not, I was thinking of *your* team." He gestured toward them. "I see that some of the girls have quit. I'm surprised more didn't. This is the last game. Take a chance. See what happens."

How would her team feel about a certain loss? "I'll think about it after I talk to the girls."

"Great." His smile was approving. Ivy savored the feeling. "Are we still on for pizza at CAPS after the game? I told the paper to forward our calls there."

Ivy grinned. *That* she didn't need to think about. "You bet. Don't forget the pictures and trophies."

The referee blew her whistle. Ivy and Rick formally shook hands and returned to the sidelines.

Studying her roster with the playing-position assignments, Ivy thought about Rick's suggestion. Why not? She could always return to her plan if the game went badly. "How about choosing your own positions today and everybody plays at least two quarters?" she asked, expecting to hear a chorus of groans and protests, not cheering and jumping.

Even the reluctant ballerinas, who took every opportunity to let Ivy know they were being forced to continue soccer, were laughing and clapping their hands.

"You know we might not win this game," Ivy began, but her team didn't seem to care. Definitely didn't care. Might never have cared.

Tears she couldn't blame on the wind blurred her eyes at the sight of her gleeful team. To them, winning wasn't as important as playing the game. Ivy had tried so hard to give them a taste of adult competition. They hadn't liked it any more than she did now.

"What position do I play, Coach Ivy?" Ruth Ann danced around her.

Ivy swallowed. "What position do you want to play?" she managed to ask.

"Goalie!"

"Goalie it is, then."

"Thank goodness," said Lanie, whose regular position it was. "I hated playing goalie."

Ivy called to Ruth Ann, reminding her to put on the goalie's special identifying shirt. The little girl was being hugged by her parents, who usually attended the games. As Ivy watched, Ruth Ann's father reached into his briefcase, the one he always brought with him. A workaholic, Ivy had thought. Now she saw that it wasn't a briefcase at all, but a video-camera case. He taped Ruth Ann putting on her goalie's shirt.

Looking at their proud, eager faces, Ivy felt sick. Horribly sick, the deep nauseating sickness that came with the realization she'd made a huge mistake.

The girls hadn't cared about their team winning as much as they cared about playing. She'd thought she'd encourage them to work harder by rewarding the best ones. Instead, she'd only discouraged the less talented players.

A subdued Ivy assigned the remaining positions by asking what the girls wanted to play.

A benign referee allowed frequent substitutions during the periods as giggling girls changed places.

A delighted Rick watched his team score more goals than they had all season.

Ivy lost count and so, it seemed, did everyone else.

After the game, Rick walked over and draped an arm around her shoulders as she stood and watched the jumping, laughing girls. "I thought it was important for them to win," she said. "You know, team effort and all that."

"Winning is important." Rick smiled down at her. "It feels good, too."

Ivy made a face. "Don't you dare say winning isn't everything. It's usually the winner who says it."

Rick grinned and squeezed her shoulders.

"I messed up their whole soccer season, didn't I?"

"Absolutely not!" Rick said, shaking his head. "They wouldn't have been able to play at all if you hadn't volunteered."

Ivy sighed. "I guess that makes me feel a little better."

"It should make you feel a lot better. Look." He pointed to the teams, milling around and drinking from juice boxes. "Do they look like they're holding a grudge?"

Ivy shook her head. "They look hungry."

"Well, c'mon. Let's go eat pizza."

The teams' high spirits carried over to their pizza party at the CAPS office. Rick and Ivy presented trophies to each girl and in turn received plaques with their team's picture.

The engraving under the photograph read, Ivy's League. Ivy studied it, silently apologizing to the three girls in the picture who'd quit after the photograph was taken.

"Neat, huh?" Rick looked over her shoulder. "Let me show you where I'm hanging mine." He gestured for her to follow him.

They left the noisy girls in the snack bar and went down the hall. In the reception area, he indicated the wall between the window and the door leading to the conference rooms.

Ivy nodded her agreement. "Only the first of many civic awards, I'm sure," she commented lightly.

"You'll probably gather a few yourself," Rick responded. He went through the door and reappeared at Lincoln's desk. "I wonder if Linc keeps a hammer and nails somewhere in here?"

He poked through a few drawers, then opened the supply cabinet. Ivy propped her elbows on the windowsill. "What are you going to do with all your free time now that you aren't coaching?" She meant it to sound like a casual query, although it was anything but.

When she saw him smile, she knew she hadn't fooled him. "We'll have to date like regular people, won't we?"

She felt her face heat with an annoying blush. "I'm not asking you to take me out and spend money on me or anything."

Rick closed the cabinet, without finding hammer or nails, and leaned on the opposite side of the window. He wore a serious expression. "How are you doing at separating the professional *us* from the personal *us?* I know I'm having a hard time."

His admission endeared him to Ivy. "You're doing great."

"Well, you'd just better make sure I'm not around when some jerk in a locker room gets out of line. I can't promise I won't deck him."

Ivy laughed. "And I can't promise I won't let you."

The chirp of the telephone interrupted their shared laughter.

Still chuckling, Rick answered it, seemed surprised and handed the receiver to Ivy.

"Hello?" She looked questioningly at Rick, but he shook his head and shrugged.

One of the Colt players was calling, quite put out and, lucky for Ivy, extremely vocal.

She grabbed for scratch paper. Rick didn't leave. Extremely conscious of his interested gaze, Ivy suggested that she interview the player in person.

"Anything important?" Rick asked the moment she hung up the phone.

"Oh—" Ivy tried for nonchalance "—developments in a story I've been working on. I have to leave now. I'm due in Fort Worth at three, and I have to run an errand first. Let me say goodbye to the girls."

She risked a glance at his face. He did not look satisfied with her explanation. As quickly as she could, Ivy slipped away.

Texas Central College, home of the Colts, was about an hour's drive from Austin. Ivy felt guilty during the entire drive and berated herself for it. *She'd* discovered this story. She'd also given Rick the message from Coach Collin and it had nothing to do with anything she was writing about.

She wouldn't share this information with any other *Globe* reporter and Rick wouldn't expect her to. She wanted—needed—to research this story all on her own so Rick would see she was a competent reporter. Maybe not the best in the locker room, but competent.

When she broke this story, she'd be an established reporter at last. Rick would be free to accept the position with *International Sports,* if he chose.

Life would be just great.

CHAPTER TEN

THE RUNNING BACK must have called her during half-time, Ivy realized when she pulled into the Colts' stadium and found a game in progress. Something—or someone—was really bothering him.

After parking her car, she rested her head on the steering wheel. The situation called for another trip to the Colts' locker room.

This time Rick wouldn't be around.

If the player hadn't sounded so urgently secretive, Ivy would've asked him to call her at the *Globe* instead of driving all this way. But now that she had a contact of her own, she had to accommodate him. She'd wanted contacts, right?

The postgame chatter in the locker room was muffled and subdued, especially since the Colts had allowed a healthy halftime lead to evaporate. They'd won—barely.

Ivy stepped inside and stood near the door, not charging forward the way she usually did. Most of the other reporters were from the local media. Ivy was one of the few outsiders.

Today, Saturday, was a big Conference-game day, and the major Texas publications had sent their staff to cover those games. The Colts weren't Conference members and thus didn't rate extensive press coverage.

In fact, because of their soccer match, she and Rick had missed the noon games they might normally have covered. Impatiently, she glanced at her watch. If she didn't find player number thirty-two quickly, she wouldn't arrive in time for the three-o'clock kickoff in Fort Worth.

"Ms. Hall?" A muscular youth tapped her on the arm. "I'm Jeremy."

Several other players huddled near Jeremy. All wore identical looks of distress.

"Brett is going to turn pro after this season," Jeremy announced, glancing over his shoulder. "We found out during halftime."

Brett—the talented junior quarterback.

"Yeah, he's signed with some pushy agent," added another player. "Now he thinks he's too good for us."

Ivy scribbled furiously. Texas Central would be losing both quarterbacks. No wonder the players were upset. The team would be considerably weakened.

"We think Coach Collin talked him into turning pro. Why would Coach do that?"

Jeremy expressed his hope that if Ivy wrote the story from their point of view, somehow Brett could be stopped from throwing away his remaining year of eligibility.

Ivy had her doubts, but she thanked the young players profusely and followed a stream of reporters into an interview room. There Brett sat, already showered and dressed. No more ordinary locker-room interviews for the new star. From now on, he'd hold press conferences.

A man wearing a hat stood at his side. *A pushy agent.* Rudy Allen. She should've known. Rudy always could pick the winners.

He did all the talking, answering questions while Brett smiled.

Ivy had heard it all before. She crept quietly back into the locker room, searching for Coach Collin. She found him in his office.

"Well, look who's here. The girl reporter." Coach Collin reached for a cigar and, Ivy suspected, lit it just to annoy her. He smiled and leaned back in his chair.

She didn't like his smile, but she asked him a question anyway. "What plans do you have for the team next year now that both Taylor and Brett are leaving?"

"We'll be in the process of rebuilding...."

He expounded on his plans and Ivy wrote, hearing nothing out of the ordinary. Any coach in his position would have to rebuild. No coach would admit that his next team didn't stand a chance of having a winning season. Still, he was much more talkative than she'd expected him to be. Perhaps he enjoyed torturing her with cigar smoke.

"Did you encourage Brett Carson to enter the pro-football draft?"

He squinted at her. "Now, why would I do that?"

Urging a talented player to leave college didn't make sense to Ivy, either. "Are you aware of any resentment among the rest of the Colts?" Ivy tried to couch the question in general terms so as not to betray Jeremy and the others.

Coach Collin barked a laugh. "They wouldn't be human if they weren't jealous. Teach them to try harder."

"But isn't their playing responsible for the success of your quarterbacks? Shouldn't they receive some sort of recognition?"

The smile was wiped from Coach Collin's face. "I coached those quarterbacks, and don't you forget it, Missy. And make sure you learn to spell my name right. You'll be hearing it a lot. You know why?"

He seemed to expect a negative response, so Ivy shook her head.

"Because we're changing our offense." He gestured with the cigar. "I haven't told anybody this—" Ivy's heartbeat accelerated "—but we've got some players transferring in from two junior colleges, and they're going to make everybody sit up and take notice."

As he talked, Ivy wrote in a frenzied scrawl. Now *this* was news. The other reporters were concentrating on the newest pro candidate, and only Ivy was talking to the coach.

Her sweaty hand ached when Coach Collin stopped talking. Ivy thanked him for the interview, trying not to gush. Then she ran to a bank of pay phones, digging coins out of her purse. Her fingers shook so much she had difficulty shoving a quarter into the proper slot. Loose change bounced at her feet.

Coach Collin's new offense. A breaking story! One that couldn't wait—maybe even a *Globe* exclusive.

"Boyd Harris, please. Ivy Hall." She gulped great breaths of clean, smoke-free air, not wanting to sound as if she was panting with excitement, which was exactly what she was doing. When her editor came on the line, she was ready.

Her story—her exclusive story—would be in Monday's issue of the *Globe.* Ivy gave a little hop of glee.

The rest of the day passed in a blur. Though it was nearing midnight when she drove back from the final game of the day, Ivy proceeded straight to the *Globe* building. She'd managed to interview Brett Carson after her call to Mr. Harris, and she wanted to type up her story while her notes were fresh.

And, to be honest, she wanted to gloat to Rick, if he happened to be hanging around.

This story was just what she needed to boost her self-confidence. She'd followed a hunch and it had paid off. She hadn't asked for help from anyone. Mr. Harris had been extremely complimentary.

Ivy pulled into the parking lot of the *Globe* building, feeling as if she finally belonged. For the first time since she'd interned as a student, she didn't feel she'd made the wrong career choice. Charged with energy, she dashed up four flights of stairs, rather than waiting for the elevator.

She was going to make it. She may not be running her own successful business like her sisters, but she could hold her head up at any family gathering.

Without a word to her co-workers, she sat at her computer station and began composing a story about talented quarterbacks and how a small Texas college would cope with their departure.

Midnight came and went and the room emptied. Ivy was oblivious to everything except the blinking amber cursor.

When a finger tapped her shoulder, she yelped.

"Sorry I startled you, Ivy." Mr. Harris took an awkward step back and stuffed his hands into his pockets. "Would you come with me, please?"

He looked solemn. Ivy saved her file and followed him to his office. Her hands became cold and clammy. When Mr. Harris opened the door for her, Ivy saw that he wasn't alone. Rick was with him.

A Rick who sat staring at the floor, resting his elbows on his knees.

She made a small sound, and he shifted his head, looking at her with a flat, bleak gaze.

Mr. Harris had walked behind his desk, but he didn't sit. Instead, he stared at papers littering the smooth top

Something was horribly wrong. Why didn't anyone speak?

Eventually, Ivy's editor scooted two pieces of paper toward the edge of his desk and sat down, mutely gesturing toward a battered folding chair.

It squeaked as Ivy sat.

"About the article you called in, Ivy..." He stopped and cleared his throat.

"Just tell me what's wrong." Obviously something was.

"What were your sources?"

Ivy outlined the events that led to her breaking the story.

"When did you talk to Coach Collin?"

"This afternoon. I walked directly out of his office to the phones and called you."

Mr. Harris shook his head.

Rick, behind her, muttered something. When she turned to face him, he said, "Sonny Collin has accepted the job of head coach for the Miami Panthers next year."

She forgot to breathe. "He'll be coaching the Panthers?" She hadn't even known the Panthers were looking for a new coach.

Rick nodded. So did Mr. Harris.

"He's called a press conference for Monday morning at ten—just after the *Globe* will hit the stands," her editor said. "It's lucky we found out in advance."

Ivy felt her mouth drop open. "That... He—" She was stunned. "He talked on and on about his rebuilding program for the Colts, knowing all the time he wouldn't be their coach next year," she told Rick in disbelief. "His new offensive plan... He knew I'd write about it. He meant for me to make a fool of myself."

"Most unfortunate," Mr. Harris said. "We won't be able to run your story, you realize. However, Rick was able to provide us with an exclusive interview, so at the same time the rest of the media learns of Coach Collin's decision, the public can read about it in the *Globe*. Well done, Rick."

Rick? *Rick.*

Ivy turned to him, mutely asking for an explanation when she really felt like howling and kicking and throwing a world-class tantrum.

Rick exhaled audibly. "I talked with Sonny after you left CAPS."

And stole her story. Ivy stared at him. "You answered the telephone. You knew that a player from the Colts called me, didn't you?" She was proud of her voice. No shaking. No tears.

"Yes."

At least he didn't lie or apologize. "You knew I was driving to the stadium."

"I figured it out."

"And then made a few phone calls."

"Just one."

How modest. "And scooped me."

"And scooped you." His voice was a gruff whisper.

"Did you set me up, too?" Filing an erroneous story was a disaster. A hideous disaster. Maybe a career-ending disaster. If the *Globe* had printed her article . . .

But that wasn't Ivy's greatest concern at the moment.

"I did not set you up!" Rick maintained adamantly. "Sonny thought of that without any help from me."

"Why would he do that?" She heard the bewilderment in her voice. "Why would he set me up?"

Rick heaved a sigh. "He's never liked women in the locker room."

It had come down to that. Again.

She and Rick gazed at each other. Rick's expression held regret mixed with defiance. She didn't know what was in hers.

Ivy swiveled in her seat to face a silent and acutely uncomfortable Boyd Harris. She reached for her story. "I was able to interview Brett Carson, the junior who's turning pro, and some of his disgruntled teammates. I can slant the article toward them—the guys left behind—and it could make a good companion piece to Rick's article." How professional she sounded. She'd pat herself on the back later. After she finished crying.

Silence. Mr. Harris stared at his thumbs. So did Rick. "What's the matter?" She glanced from one to the other.

"Uh..." Mr. Harris began. "Excellent idea. However, Rick has provided us with an article on Brett Carson. It seems that the Miami Panthers are looking to draft a quarterback. Brett works well with Sonny Collin."

Ivy closed her eyes in a slow blink. "Rick's been busy." She stood, surprised to find her knees steady. "Then I'll write up the Fort Worth game—unless Rick was able to beam himself there, as well."

"No, uh, that's fine, Ivy." Mr Harris sounded so relieved Ivy wanted to laugh. Hysterically. Maniacally.

She walked out of the editor's office, closed the glass door carefully and headed toward her desk. Rick followed right behind her. He wasn't quite as careful with the door.

Ivy ignored him, though she was aware of his every movement. She sat at her computer, opened a new file and got to work. If she kept busy, she wouldn't fall apart. Right now, it was terribly important that she not fall apart.

Rick sighed and rolled his chair across the aisle. "Say something."

"Congratulations."

"No—something about what's happened."

Ivy didn't answer.

"We need to talk."

"Ha!"

"Okay, yell at me, then."

"So you can feel better?" She glared at him.

"I don't feel bad now," he shot back.

Ivy gasped, then deliberately closed her mouth and turned back to the computer. Amazingly, she didn't feel like crying. She wasn't blushing and didn't feel particularly angry. Maybe this was cold fury. She rather liked the elegant sound of being coldly furious after suffering a betrayal.

"It's one o'clock in the morning, Ivy."

"So leave." Ivy typed furiously. It wasn't the world's greatest copy, but she hoped to preserve the illusion that she wasn't shattered by Rick's betrayal.

"I want to see that you make it home okay."

"Feeling a teensy bit guilty?"

Rick reached over and covered her hands on the keyboard. The extra weight depressed a key that filled the screen with *K*s until the computer beeped in protest. He released her hands and she put them in her lap.

"I treated you the way I would have any other reporter. That's what *you* wanted."

"You mean you steal stories from everybody here?"

Rick's jaw clenched. "I didn't steal your story. You didn't have one to steal."

"That's right, rub it in."

"Ivy!" He inhaled and exhaled forcibly. Twice. "I went to Boyd's office tonight to see if you'd filed the Collin story. If you had, I would have pulled mine."

Was she supposed to feel better? "Would you have done that for anybody else?"

"Probably not."

"Well, why not? Don't you have any professional ethics?" Her cold fury was changing to white-hot anger.

Rick was clearly becoming angry, too. "You want to talk ethics? Okay, what tipped you off about the Colts, anyway? Perhaps a certain phone call? To *me?*"

"I wouldn't have answered that call if you'd been at your desk where you should have been, instead of hiding out at CAPS avoiding me!"

"Are you telling me you can't be trusted?"

How had he managed to make this whole thing seem like her fault? "I gave you the message. You said he was calling about something else. I broke the story on my own. I spent hours calling players and trainers. And you—" she glared at him "—you make one phone call and the coach tells all."

"Sonny Collin is a friend of mine! Of course he'd confide in me before he'd tell you anything."

"And then help you out by lying to me?"

"I hope you believe I knew nothing about that."

Of course she knew Rick wouldn't have set her up. Integrity oozed from his pores. "Maybe I do—" Ivy tossed her head "—and maybe I don't."

Rick looked as though he wanted to strangle her. "I've dreaded this. Ever since we started seeing each other, I knew it was only a matter of time before we'd clash over something and you'd get mad."

Ivy gritted her teeth. "Let's not downplay your part in this affair."

Rick ran both hands through his hair. "Ivy, you can't ignore the fact that you're female. Believe me, no one else can."

Ivy bit her lower lip, nodding slowly. "This is how you've justified your help to me—the fact that I'm female."

"Sonny wouldn't have out-and-out lied to a male reporter."

Ivy had suspected that, but hearing Rick voice it made her angry. "So he's a world-class jerk."

"And he's declared war. What are you going to do about it?"

"I don't want to fight with anybody." She wouldn't stoop to the coach's level.

"If you don't fight back, you'll never get a straight interview with him again."

"Big deal, the Colts aren't exactly front-page news."

Rick regarded her steadily. "He isn't going to be with the Colts, remember? He'll be coaching the Miami Panthers."

Now she felt like crying.

"And to be honest, it would surprise me if this is the only instance of harassment and prejudice you'll experience in your career."

Despair replaced what was left of her elegantly cold anger.

Rick cleared his throat. "If you aren't prepared to fight that prejudice, then you're in the wrong business."

First Billie, now Rick.

Ivy's image of herself as a successful reporter, a successful career woman, was crumbling. She'd thought that was what she'd wanted. What she was supposed to want. She'd seen her sisters grow in their careers; it was unthinkable that she wouldn't have a career, too.

Whether or not she wanted one.

She quickly muffled *that* tiny inner voice. The Hall sisters had careers—period.

Ivy summoned a smile. Time to let Rick know it would take a lot more to run her out of the business. "Fighting prejudice is one thing. Fighting you is something else."

Okay, it was a gentle nudge and an opening for him to apologize for horning in on her story. If Rick hadn't investigated the reason a Colts player had phoned her, none of this would have happened.

Ivy discounted the fact that the *Globe* would have then published an erroneous story. If Rick hadn't spoken to the coach before she did, the man probably wouldn't have misled her.

RICK KNEW he was supposed to reassure her. But he wasn't going to apologize for what he'd done.

He wanted to gather her in his arms and tell her this would never happen again. But that would be lying.

"Ivy, we're competing professionally." He drew a deep breath and forced himself to continue. "If I have the opportunity, I'll scoop you again."

The death of her innocence was horrible to watch. As the seconds passed and she fully understood what he was telling her, the wounded look left her eyes. Bitterness filled them. A bitterness Rick knew would sour their personal relationship.

"I see."

"Just as I would scoop any reporter." She bowed her head. "Just as I would expect you to scoop me if you could."

She glanced up. "But that isn't likely in this market, is it, Rick?"

"What's that supposed to mean?"

"I think I understand why those other reporters left. They moved on because you're so firmly entrenched here. You're a hometown hero. Everyone knows you, has coached you or played with you." She shook her head. "How can I compete with you? How can anyone?"

"I'm not going to apologize for a lifetime of contacts."

"I don't expect you to. But that's here in Austin. Just what kind of reporter would you be in New York?"

"Better than you." She flinched, and he immediately regretted his harsh words.

"But opportunities would be a lot more even," she insisted stubbornly.

Rick felt his anger grow. "*You* made a mistake and now you're searching for somebody to blame it on."

"I blew it, but you were right there to take advantage, weren't you? You don't want me to succeed. You want to run me off."

Rick thought he'd explode. "Women!"

"Now we hear your true feelings."

He closed his eyes and silently counted to ten. "Ivy, it's very late. This discussion has deteriorated into a personal attack, and I told you we'd have to separate our professional and personal lives. Let me drive you home."

"No. I've got work to do."

"Leave it." He smiled. "Let's go kiss and make up." He reached over and turned off her monitor.

"How dare you!" Rick had never seen her this angry. "And after what happened, how can you expect me to just . . . just . . ." She gestured vaguely.

"Kiss and make up?" The expression on her face chilled him. "Because what happens professionally isn't supposed to affect us personally, remember?"

Her fist slammed her desk top, startling them both. "How can it not? How can you kiss me one minute and stab me in the back the next? And then tell me you'd do it again?" She shook her head. "I thought I could separate my feelings, but I can't."

Unfortunately, Rick couldn't separate his feelings, either. Of course, he'd never thought he could. "It's late," he said into the silence. His command of the language had deserted him.

"If you want to leave, then go. Just go!"

And never come back, he heard, though she didn't say the words. "Ivy." It was more a call to the Ivy she'd been, than the Ivy she was now. He should take his own advice and get some sleep. He'd done enough damage for one night. "Be careful driving home."

She squeezed her eyes shut. He couldn't be certain, but he thought he saw a tear leaking out.

It would embarrass her if he stayed any longer. With a sigh, Rick walked out of the newsroom.

THE SOUND of his footsteps died away before Ivy opened her eyes and wiped the corners.

Not only wasn't Rick sorry, he'd do it again. He'd painted a combative picture of her future as a sportswriter. She would have to remain ever vigilant for betrayal or the chance to betray someone else. Against prejudice and false information. She looked down her chosen career path and didn't like what she saw. She'd never get used to it. Never.

Writing and sports had been her two loves—until she met Rick. Combining sports and writing had been difficult, but mixing in her feelings for Rick had been a disaster.

She didn't want this stupid job. She wanted Rick.

So why did she have the job—instead of Rick?

Ivy finished her article on the Fort Worth game and turned off her monitor.

Light glowed from Boyd Harris's office. Either maintenance was cleaning or he was still there.

As she watched, the light blinked off and Mr. Harris emerged. He scanned the newsroom, waving when he saw her.

"Mr. Harris!"

He waited as she walked toward him between desks. "Ivy, there's no need for you to be here this late. Go on home."

"I will. First, I want to apologize for filing an erroneous story."

He held up both hands, warding off her apology. "These things happen."

Ivy wondered if he'd be so understanding if the *Globe* had already gone to press. "So I've been told. In fact, I've been told I can expect more of the same."

"It won't be as bad as all that." The editor looked tired.

"For me, it will. That's why I want to quit."

He smiled, shaking his head. Obviously he didn't believe she was serious. "No, no. That's not necessary."

"I think it is."

"Not at two in the morning," he said with a pained expression. "Go home and sleep on it."

Ivy took a deep breath. "I find things become very clear at two in the morning. I'll go home now. But I won't change my mind."

CHAPTER ELEVEN

"IVY CRY."

"Yes, Aunt Ivy's crying." Ivy sniffed and wrestled an angel Christmas ornament away from two-and-a-half-year-old Nicholas. "Here, play with this." She handed him a blue rubber Cookie Monster from the set of Sesame Street tree ornaments.

He chewed on the figure, tried to take the head off, then cast it aside and dug in the ornament box.

Today was Thanksgiving. Four days earlier, when Mr. Harris had told her to go home, she'd suddenly had a vision of her family home. Her tiny one-bedroom apartment with its dingy walls had never been home.

Although the impressive Dallas mansion where she'd grown up belonged to her sister and brother-in-law now, it was still home, and Ivy found plenty of space to hide. She'd buried herself in one of the many upstairs bedrooms, inventorying ornaments.

Holly had welcomed the extra help as she geared up for the busiest time of the year for her Christmas decorating service, Deck the Halls. Ivy was an old hand at packing Christmas-tree decorations. Nicholas, her nephew, "helped," too.

When she'd arrived home, Holly, with rare but welcome sensitivity, had not questioned her. But now it was time to face the world again. Ivy couldn't pretend she was on vacation forever. Even the most liberal of employers didn't give an entire week's leave at Thanksgiving.

Ivy had returned to the *Globe* with a formal letter of resignation later on the Sunday morning after her debacle. She hadn't slept at all, spending the early-morning hours packing.

Mr. Harris had insisted that she keep her press credentials and offered to buy any feature articles she wrote, telling her she was the best feature writer he had. Ivy clung to the praise on the drive from Austin to Dallas. If Mr. Harris liked her features, maybe other editors would, as well. Perhaps she could support herself free-lancing. She just knew she couldn't face the locker-room pressure cooker again.

Thus, she was able to arrive at Holly's in a positive frame of mind, which deteriorated rapidly as the days passed with no word from Rick. She'd left him a short note telling him she'd quit and gone home. Writing the words had made her feel like such a failure she hadn't been able to add more. But she'd expected some sort of response by now—a phone call, even.

Nothing. Obviously his feelings for her weren't as strong as hers were for him.

"Nicholas, what is it with you men?"

The little boy looked at her, grinned and held up a yellow ornament. "Big Bud."

"Big Bird," Ivy agreed.

Nicholas discarded Big Bird and continued exploring the ornament box.

"I mean, I thought he loved me. He never said the words, but I could tell...."

Nicholas looked at her solemnly, with Holly's eyes topped by Adam's trademark black eyebrows. He reached out and dropped a green-and-silver blob in her lap. "Ahka."

Ivy shook her head. "Sorry. Oscar's not the man for me."

But Rick was. And she'd thrown him over for a job she didn't even want. She'd said terrible things. Accused him of terrible things.

And regretted every word.

Ivy drew a deep breath. The air was redolent with the smell of the roasting turkey they'd eat tonight, assuming she'd be able to choke down any food at all. She closed her eyes.

"Ivy cry."

"I know." She sniffed. "Aunt Ivy's being ridiculous." She gathered Nicholas in a tight hug that made him squirm. "You know what? Aunt Ivy is tired of crying."

She rose to her feet and held out her hand to her nephew. "C'mon, Nicholas. Let's go find your mom and see if she needs help with dinner."

They found Holly in her office, scheduling Christmas-tree-decorating jobs. Holly took one look at her and sighed. "Ivy, I've had it. You've been moping around here all week and I've been really proud of myself for not prying, but it's time you talked about it—him. Only a man can cause this kind of suffering."

Ivy started to deny that anything was wrong, but couldn't lie, not to her sister and not to herself. "Oh, Holly!" she wailed. "I've ruined my life!"

While Nicholas sat on the desk and removed caps from all his mother's pens and markers, a watery Ivy told her about Rick and her job and their terrible argument.

"You quit?" Holly asked.

Ivy had dreaded her sister's reaction. "Yes." Hall sisters didn't quit. Ever.

Holly nodded. "From what you've said, it didn't seem like the right job for you."

Maybe Holly didn't understand. "I don't think it's the right *career* for me. I don't think *any* career is the right career for me. I don't want to become hard and aggressive. I can't." Ivy waited for the lecture, the lecture about Hall sisters and family honor and never quitting.

Holly grabbed Nicholas, who'd decided to chew on a marker. Green drool stained his chin. "You'll find something else."

That was it? "I don't want to find anything else!" There, her horrible secret was out. Ivy began crying again.

"What *do* you want?"

Her sister's calmly asked question quieted Ivy. Grabbing a tissue from the box on Holly's desk, Ivy collided with the multicolored hand of her nephew. He smiled at her, and the sweetness of it pierced her heart.

She wanted a home and babies. Rick's babies. She wanted to bake cookies, be a room mother and drive in the car pool. She wanted to coach soccer again and get it right this time. She wanted to spend her life cheering Rick's successes and mourning his losses. She wanted time to write thoughtful, in-depth feature stories.

"You love him, don't you?" Holly gazed at her with an understanding smile. "You aren't angry about losing your job. You're upset about losing Rick."

Ivy hiccuped. "He's the most wonderful, caring—"

"Shh. Of course he is. So call him," Holly said matter-of-factly. "Talk. Work things out." She checked her watch. "You've got time right now."

"Now? I don't even know where he is."

Holly rolled her eyes and plunked the telephone down in front of Ivy. "Today's Thanksgiving. Either he's at home or he's working." She hoisted Nicholas onto her hip. "Maybe *I* should have been the reporter," she said as she left her office.

Rick was working. In fact, he was covering a game at Texas Stadium, right here in Dallas. With her sister's encouragement and an admonition that dinner would be ready in an hour, Ivy drove to Texas Stadium.

She searched for him everywhere, finally ending up at the locker-room entrance, ready to barge in and declare her love in front of a team of sweaty players if necessary.

It wasn't necessary. Rick wasn't there.

TRADITIONAL THANKSGIVING smells assaulted Ivy the instant she opened the door to the kitchen.

"It's about time!" Holly greeted her. "The turkey was done forty-five minutes ago. It'll probably fall off the bones. So? What happened?"

Ivy, stomach roiling, tried to smile.

One glance at her face and her sister enveloped her in a hug, then handed her a whisk and nudged her toward the stove. Ivy cried into the gravy.

"Try to find him tomorrow," Holly suggested, carrying dishes of food into the dining room.

Ivy trailed after her. "It won't do any good." Holly shot her a look that clearly told Ivy her patience was nearing an end.

A burning smell wafted into the room. The gravy. Great. She couldn't do anything right.

Holly ran to the kitchen and grabbed the saucepan off the stove. She gazed into the bubbling, black-bottomed mess and scraped off the top layer of gravy. "Ivy, go watch TV until dinner is ready. I'm sure there's a football game on somewhere.''

"Football?" Ivy shrieked. "My life is over and you tell me to watch football? I don't care about football or writing about football or anyone who's playing football! I don't care if I never see another football game!''

Holly gestured with the saucepan before dunking it under water. "Ivy, dear, if you don't care about football, then this is true love.''

Ivy sniffed, then straightened her shoulders. "I exaggerated his feelings for me and mine for him. I'll get over it. This time next week, I won't even remember his name.''

"Uh-huh." Holly obviously saw through her lie.

"I will, Holly. Honestly, this was just an infatuation on my part.''

"Nonsense. You love him. Just keep after him until he breaks down and admits he loves you, too.''

"It's not as simple as that.''

"Sure, it is," Holly said, dismissing Ivy's days of agony.

Her sister didn't understand.

The doorbell chimed as Ivy slumped into a chair, feeling drained. Her heart was broken. Holly, mired in happy domesticity, couldn't remember what a broken heart felt like.

"Adam must have forgotten his keys. He took Nicholas for a walk." Holly sent her a harried look. "Could you...?''

Ivy nodded and forced herself to walk to the front door. It wasn't locked. "Adam," she said, opening the door, "it's not—" She broke off, staring.

Rick stared back.

Her heart began beating wildly, not broken, after all. "Rick," she mouthed, all the air gone from her lungs. She was afraid to blink, afraid that if she did, he'd disappear.

"May I come in?" he asked when she didn't move.

Wordlessly, Ivy held the door open wider. He brushed past her, closing it himself.

It really was Rick. She searched his face, noting the shadows under his eyes and the lines bracketing his mouth.

"Rick—"

"Ivy—"

They spoke at the same time, breaking off uncomfortably. Rick stared down at a small, plastic-wrapped bundle in his hands, then thrust it toward her. "Here."

Her fingers closed around a lump. "What is this?"

"Genetically, it's Rock Cornish hen, but let's pretend it's crow." He raised his eyebrows in a rueful expression and shoved his hands into his pockets.

Ivy smiled for the first time in five days. "You're going to eat crow?"

Rick nodded. "Groveling is easier with props."

Hope flickered within Ivy, but she'd hoped before. And been disappointed before. Her smile was cautious. An apology was not a declaration of everlasting love, but at least they'd be speaking to each other again.

They both eyed the small bundle Ivy clutched. She swallowed, waiting.

"Ivy, I've been—"

"A jerk," interrupted a voice from the dining room behind them. Holly stood there, her brown eyes challenging Rick's.

Ivy groaned.

"You must be Holly," he said.

"And you must be the man who's made my sister cry for the last week." With a frosty glare, Holly thunked a bowl of mashed potatoes onto the table.

Ivy gritted her teeth. "Holly!" she warned.

Holly shook a finger at them. "Y'all have five minutes to kiss and make up."

"Holly!" How humiliating. How typical.

"I've created a culinary masterpiece carefully timed to be at its peak half an hour ago." Holly gestured to the table. "I now have burnt, lumpy gravy, rapidly cooling vegetables and a melting jelly mold. I suggest you skip the apology, kiss her and propose. Then you can stay for dinner."

"Hol-ly!" Ivy squeezed her eyes shut, hoping that if she wished hard enough, she'd disappear. Or her sister would.

"Thank you for your suggestions," she heard Rick say dryly. "But I was doing quite nicely on my own."

"Ha!" Holly walked toward the kitchen. "You brought her a dead bird. If that's your idea of romance, no wonder she's been crying for days." Mercifully, Holly vanished into the kitchen.

"It's already cooked!" Rick called after her.

"Good," they heard. "It may be the only thing left that's edible."

Ivy prayed for a natural disaster. Even an unnatural one. Cautiously she looked up at Rick.

He gazed at the door through which Holly had disappeared. "You know, your sister's bossy, but she's right about—"

"Three minutes!" Holly called.

"She's also getting on my nerves," he muttered.

Ivy exhaled slowly. "She tends to do that."

They smiled at each other, tentative smiles, shaky at the corners.

"I'm sorry...." they said together, then laughed. Rick reached for Ivy just as the door opened and Adam and Nicholas bounded in. Ivy nearly screamed in frustration. Nicholas continued running through the dining room into the kitchen, but Adam stopped, training his blue gaze first on Ivy, then Rick.

The two men took each other's measure as Ivy, teeth clenched, introduced them. Adam, always able to size up a situation quickly and accurately, gave Rick The Look. Powerful men had backed down from The Look. Even Holly didn't fool around with The Look.

Adam offered his hand and Rick shook it. No one said anything. The two men continued to study each other, silently communicating on some male level. Then, incredibly, Ivy's brother-in-law winked at her. "A piece of advice, Rick—when dealing with the women in this family, act quickly and decisively." Adam started toward the kitchen. "And don't give them a chance to think. Thinking gets them into trouble."

Ivy made a strangled sound. "Do you suppose anyone has ever died of embarrassment?" She couldn't face Rick. After this, she might not even be able to face Adam and Holly.

Rick chuckled softly. "I do love you, Ivy. Your family has already figured that out."

Her eyes widened and met his. For one glorious moment, her heart soared before plummeting. He'd finally said he loved her, but only after her family had implied they'd expected nothing less. Ivy moaned. "Not that there's any pressure on you or anything."

"No pressure," Rick said, taking her hands in his. His thumbs grazed her knuckles back and forth. "I was afraid that you'd hang up on me if I phoned, so I drove here to apologize—once I found out where you were." A smile hovered around his lips. "I'm lucky I got in the door. Your family makes a strong defensive line."

Ivy rolled her eyes. "Don't you mean offensive?"

"They love you." He took a step closer. "*I* love you."

He'd said it again. Once might have been an impulse, but twice? Feeling the sting of tears, Ivy blinked rapidly. "Do you really mean it?" she asked, hearing her voice crack.

He squeezed her hands. Hard. "Yes, Ivy. For the record, I really mean it."

"Oh, Rick!" The tears spilled over. "I've been so miserable!" she wailed, and was instantly pulled close to him. "I thought I'd lost you! I said such awful things. I've never been in love before. I don't know the rules."

Rick laughed and rocked her from side to side. "I don't think there are any rules—except that at some point, you're supposed to tell me you love me, too."

"I just did." She wound her arms beneath the leather jacket and buried her face in his sweater.

He began to stroke her hair. "I never meant for you to quit your job. But as it's turned out, perhaps quitting was for the best."

"I know I was right to quit." Ivy sighed. "I couldn't compete with you by day and forget about it at night."

Rick's hand stilled. "That wasn't what I meant. You see—" he stepped back so he could see her face "—I quit, too."

"Why? You're the senior reporter."

He touched a finger to her lips. "I accepted that job with *International Sports.*"

Ivy felt the blood drain from her face. "You did? That's wonderful!" she said, attempting to be brave.

Inside, she was crying. He'd just told her he loved her. Now he was leaving. She hugged him, squeezing out selfish thoughts. "Congratulations! When do you leave for New York?"

"The first of the year." Rick's arms tightened around her. "But nothing's engraved in stone yet. I told them I'd have to think about it."

"What's there to think about? It's a fabulous opportunity." Her voice was weak.

Rick drew a deep breath. "Ivy, I want you to come with me. I can't imagine taking this on without you. I can't imagine living without you."

At his words, Ivy felt as if all the puzzle pieces of her future had finally snapped together, forming a picture. A picture with Rick.

"There are newspapers in New York," he was saying. "I know it would mean job hunting, but—"

Ivy touched a finger to his lips, echoing his gesture. "You don't have to convince me. I'll go to New York with you. I'll go anywhere with you."

Ivy watched an incredulous joy creep across Rick's face, matching her own elation. Their lips met in a searing kiss, broken by the laughter they couldn't suppress. They tried to kiss again, but their smiles got in the way.

"I don't deserve your love," Rick murmured, "but I'll try my best to make—"

A raised voice from the kitchen interrupted him. "I will *not* let my little sister go to New York and live in sin!" Holly could be clearly heard. Low murmurings indicated that Adam was trying to calm her down.

"I'm calling Laurel, that's what!" Holly went on. "If I can't talk her out of it, Laurel will."

Rick and Ivy stared at each other. "What's wrong with her?" he asked.

Ivy sighed a long-suffering sigh. "She's having a hard time accepting the fact that her little sister has grown up. And if I want to live in New York with you, then it's my decision to make, not hers."

"I don't want to come between you and your family—" he sent a puzzled look toward the kitchen "—but I got the impression she doesn't object to our getting married."

"Actually—" Ivy cleared her throat "—I don't believe we've discussed marriage."

Rick's gaze shot to her face. His eyes widened. "But that's what I meant!"

Slowly, the last knot of tension in Ivy's chest began to melt away. She relaxed. "But that's not what you said." Let Rick stew for a while. A short while.

"You *will* marry me, won't you?" he asked, the uncertainty in his voice a balm to her bruised emotions.

Ivy allowed two seconds to pass before flinging her arms around Rick's neck and squealing, "Yes!" in his ear.

Laughing, he lifted her off the ground. Ivy clung to him, feeling his heart beating against hers. It felt wonderfully right. They spun slowly together, kissing and murmuring words of love until they became aware of an audience. Rick released her and she slid to the floor in front of a censuring Holly and a stern-faced Adam.

"We're getting married!" Ivy burst out.

Relief washed over the faces of her sister and brother-in-law. "Oh, thank goodness." Holly sagged against a dining room chair. "Now we can eat."

The turkey was falling off the bones, a skin covered what was left of the gravy, and fruit cocktail floated freely in a lime green pool. Nicholas smeared mashed potatoes all over his high chair.

It was the best Thanksgiving dinner Ivy had ever eaten.

"June is such a romantic month," Holly sighed as she cut slices of pumpkin pie. "We've still got the trellis from Laurel's wedding. We'll use that. I know you'll want to tone down the table decorations. Take off a few hearts, perhaps?"

"Perhaps," Ivy murmured.

"Laurel is rather—" Holly gestured with the pie server as she explained to Rick "—flamboyant. Ivy, you don't have any, er, unusual wedding ideas I should know about, do you?"

Ivy smothered a smile. Holly hadn't recovered from the horror of Laurel's red wedding dress. People still talked about it.

"No, Holly," she reassured her sister.

"Good. I see your wedding in pastels—"

"Except that I'm not waiting until June to get married," Ivy stated.

"Of course you are." Holly resumed cutting the pie. "Laurel and I were married in June."

"But you weren't engaged in November," Ivy pointed out.

Holly didn't seem to hear. "For once, I'll have plenty of time. Nicholas, *please* try to use your fork!"

Ivy glanced at Rick. He offered an encouraging smile. She glanced at Adam, who wore his bland lawyer look. Beast! She stuck her tongue out at him.

He quickly smothered a smile and came to her rescue. "Holly, perhaps Ivy has another date in mind."

Holly looked completely surprised. "Don't be ridiculous. She just got engaged."

Adam raised an eyebrow at Ivy. That was her cue. She thought rapidly, remembering Laurel's wedding. Laurel very cleverly set her wedding a week before Nicholas's due date, hoping the impending birth would slow down her sister. A heavily pregnant Holly still tried to run the show, so Laurel, with some rather unorthodox ideas of her own, simply changed all of Holly's plans. Memories of the battle between two sisters with strong personalities made Ivy shudder.

She needed to find something to distract Holly. She reached under the table and found Rick's hand. He clasped hers supportively. As she smiled up at him, her eyes focused on the door to Holly's office across the foyer. "Merry Christmas! Deck the Halls," read the sign identifying her sister's Christmas decorating service.

Christmas. Holly's busiest time of the year. A make-it-or-break-it time for her business.

Merry Christmas.

Marry Christmas.

Ivy tugged on Rick's hand until he leaned down to hear her. "Christmas?" she whispered. "Shall we make this a *marry* Christmas?"

Rick blinked as he thought, then grinned. "Why not? You'll be the best Christmas present I ever got."

"Holly," Ivy said to her sister, but she gazed at Rick. "We're going to be married on Christmas Day."

"What?" her sister squeaked. "Christmas? *This* Christmas?"

Rick and Ivy nodded.

"Christmas!" Holly ran her fingers through her hair. "But that's in five weeks! I'm absolutely swamped at this time of year. I'll hardly be able to help you at all."

Lacing her fingers through Rick's, Ivy smiled a slow, satisfied smile. "I know."

CHAPTER TWELVE

"THAT WOMAN!" Holly glared after a cackling Billie, then closed her eyes as she visibly arranged her features in an appropriate sister-of-the-bride expression, infinitely reflected in the mirrored walls in the bride's parlor at the church. "Ivy, dear, I think you should prepare yourself for a disappointment when you view the proofs for your wedding album."

Ivy, who stood on a small pedestal so she wouldn't wrinkle her train, smiled into her bridal bouquet. This wasn't the time to inform Holly that there would be no proof viewing. Billie never allowed anyone to see photographs she considered unacceptable. She would choose the photographs and poses herself, and that was that.

Holly bent down and finished steaming the bottom of Ivy's white silk wedding dress. "I hope you won't regret your decision not to use Armando as your photographer. It was short notice, but he owes me a favor."

"This is Billie's wedding gift to us," Ivy protested mildly. "She's captured great shots in horrendous conditions. A mere wedding will be a vacation."

Holly opened her mouth to speak.

"Is that a smudge on my train?" Ivy inserted smoothly, effectively distracting her sister.

"Where?" Holly hitched her emerald green velvet dress above her knees and knelt to search the immaculate train.

Ivy twirled her bouquet of white poinsettias, marveling at how easy it was to handle Holly once she knew the trick. Too bad it had taken her twenty-four years to learn it.

Nothing was going to spoil today. Today was Christmas, and the best gift of all would be her wedding. Early that morning, she and her sisters had scrambled down the stairs and ripped open their gifts as they'd done on countless Christmases in the past.

The night before, Holly's birthday, the entire family had decorated the children's wing at the hospital. For the first time, Ivy had worn the red velvet Mrs. Claus outfit. Rick had enthusiastically donned the huge Santa Claus suit once worn by Ivy's father, and Laurel and Holly were dressed as elves. In another first, Jack, Laurel's husband, was persuaded to wear a Santa hat and a white sweatshirt with "Ho Ho Ho" printed on it, as long as Adam agreed to wear one, too. Nicholas, eyes wide, wore his red footed pajamas and eventually fell asleep in his uncle Jack's arms.

When Ivy had decided to be married on Christmas, she'd envisioned a small family gathering. Holly, in spite of the short notice, about which she complained constantly, had engineered an extravaganza.

Ivy had dreamed of shared vows in the charming stone chapel of their church. Holly had reserved the huge sanctuary.

Ivy had thought of champagne toasts back at their home. Holly had booked the grand ballroom of the Landreth Hotel.

Holly haggled, bullied and argued.

Ivy sighed, smiled and dreamed.

"Ivy, honey, *where* did you find that horrid woman?" Laurel, clad in ruby velvet, swept into the bride's parlor. "Do you know she's taking pictures in the men's dressing room?"

Ivy bestowed a serene smile on her glamorous sister. "No, but it doesn't surprise me."

Her sisters exchanged a look that said, "What would she have done without us?"

She would have been married in the small stone chapel in front of close friends and family, then eaten a glorious Christmas-night supper, been toasted with champagne, pelted with birdseed and driven away by her new husband to a destination even Holly hadn't been able to wangle out of her.

But with Holly in charge, nothing could be that simple. Arranging the details of the wedding had been Holly's gift to her, and truly, once she saw that Holly was being conservative—for Holly—Ivy hadn't minded. She held fast on just two points: Nicholas would not be ring bearer, because she knew he'd be happier sitting in the pew with his father and uncle; and Laurel would wear red and Holly would wear green.

Red was Laurel's color. Green was Holly's, and Ivy refused to discuss any alternatives. It felt good to be dictatorial, and besides, she figured that sort of behavior was expected of a bride. Not admired, just expected. In reality, the small details of her wedding were more important to her sisters than to her.

She hadn't even seen the decorations inside the church yet. Holly and Laurel said it was a surprise, and Ivy was content with that.

She did expect lots of white, though. She reached down and pulled out the full skirt of her bridal gown. Yards and yards of white silk fell from a tiny waist. And there were yards and yards of silk left over, all remaining from the decorations for Holly's first extravagant charity ball. Holly had been itching to reuse the mountains of silk, which she'd been forced to buy several years ago.

She'd first tried at Laurel's wedding, but Laurel had had other ideas. Her wedding gown had been a slinky beaded red dress with a train. It had taken months for Holly to recover from the shock. Hours after the wedding, she'd given birth to Nicholas, and she always intimated that it was the shock of having Laurel use her wedding for publicity that had precipitated the labor.

"There." Holly struggled to her feet and slowly circled Ivy, critically examining the dress for wrinkles. "You look beautiful."

"Elegantly simple." Ivy swallowed. Yes, the dressmaker had been rushed, but... Ivy stared at her reflection. The fitted bodice of her dress had a sweetheart neckline and long, tight sleeves puffed slightly at the shoulders. She'd never been one for frills, but maybe some lace, or a ruffle or two... She bit her lip. It was too late now and her dress didn't matter. Really.

She caught Laurel's gaze in the mirror.

Laurel smiled reassuringly. "The silk is your something old. And... Drumroll, Holly."

Holly did her best drumroll imitation as Laurel reached behind a closet door and unzipped a plastic bag. "This is your something new."

Holly went to help her and, as Ivy watched, billows of sparkling net appeared.

Ivy gasped. "Is that my veil?"

Her sisters nodded triumphantly.

Thousands of tiny crystals, caught in illusion netting, glistened and winked.

"I had one seamstress working on your dress and another on the veil," Holly told her.

"No wonder the dress doesn't have any decoration on it," Ivy murmured as the glittering cloud was fastened to her hair.

"You look like a snow princess," Laurel said, becoming a bit misty-eyed. "And at precisely four-thirty-seven, the sun will shine through the west windows and onto you." Laurel adjusted the rhinestone headpiece. "You'll sparkle as you say your vows."

That sounded like something her dramatic sister would think of. "I thought four-thirty-seven was an odd time for the ceremony." Ivy laughed. "But I'll sparkle even without the rhinestones."

Holly pushed back her sleeve and checked her watch. "Where is Adam?" she fretted. "He was supposed to bring Mama's necklace by now. It'll be the something borrowed."

Ivy tilted her head to one side. "Technically, it isn't borrowing."

"You're borrowing two-thirds of it," Laurel pointed out.

Ivy outstared her. For once, she had the superior height. "Anyway, I've already borrowed something *and* it's blue." She reached into the depths of her bouquet and extracted a rubber figure. "My nephew lent this to me," she said with dignity, as she held up the Cookie Monster.

"THEY'LL NEVER LET YOU IN," Jack advised Rick. "The groom isn't supposed to see the bride before the wedding."

Rick squinted into a mirror not nearly as large as the one in the bride's parlor. He ran his fingers through the short choppy layers of hair on the top of his head, then tried to pat them down. He'd never cared much about his hair, but he hoped to look his best for Ivy. "I want to see her face when she sees her present."

"I'll get her expression on film," said Billie. "Give me a sec to change lenses."

"Good idea," Adam agreed, straightening an already straight bow tie. "I'd like to have a picture of all their expressions."

Rick fluffed his layers up again, then compared his tie to Adam's. "I can't believe I actually forked out money for this thing." Sighing, he jerked it loose once more.

"As long as you were shelling out money, why didn't you spring for more material in these pants?" Lincoln crowded Rick in the mirror, his pant legs ending well above his ankles.

"Let your suspenders out," Billie instructed. "Hey, Ricky, *I* should have been best man."

Glancing in the mirror, Rick caught what appeared to be smirks on the faces of his future brothers-in-law. He raised an eyebrow. He'd known Billie a long time and wouldn't tolerate anyone making fun of her.

Adam inclined his head the barest fraction of an inch in acknowledgment.

Jack winked.

Billie's flash went off.

Rick grinned and retied his tie. Billie was one of a kind. "Hey, Linc, call if you have any trouble handling CAPS, okay?"

"*Okay.* But I'm not going to have any trouble." Lincoln settled his pants a couple of inches lower. "I've told you that at least twice a day for the past month."

"I know, but CAPS is important and I want to be sure it doesn't fall apart."

"Thanks a lot!"

Rick cuffed him on the shoulder.

"Ivy said you wanted to start a similar organization in New York," Jack commented.

Rick nodded. "Once things settle down."

"Remember, if you need a lawyer, you'll have one in the family," Adam offered, and held out his hand.

Grinning, Rick shook it.

"Gentlemen, the time draws nigh. 'Man has his will, but woman has her way.' Holmes. In other words—"

"Whose?" Rick asked dryly.

Billie shot him a watch-it look. "Let's not keep the bride waiting."

THE TAP ON THE DOOR of the bridal parlor brought expressions of relief to the faces of the two pacing matrons of honor.

Ivy wiggled her toes in her white satin pumps and sighed. She wanted to sit down. Neither Laurel nor Holly would hear of it.

"Finally!" Holly threw open the door and ushered in Jack and Adam.

Although she knew he wasn't supposed to be with them, Ivy peered over Jack's shoulder in case Rick had somehow talked his way into seeing her. She saw only Billie, whose mouth immediately formed an O.

Two soft gasps sighed into the room. Adam and Jack wore identical stunned expressions as they stared at her. Ivy had never seen Adam stunned by anything.

Was something wrong? Was the veil too much? Ivy bit her lower lip and returned their stares uncertainly.

Adam managed a slight smile and began to blink rapidly.

Jack cleared his throat. "Ivy, you look . . ."

"Like a snowflake in the moonlight," said Billie in an awed whisper.

Laurel sniffed. "There goes my mascara."

"Do you think Rick will like my dress?" Ivy asked.

Everyone just smiled until Jack cleared his throat again. "Speaking of Rick, he'd like to be here now, but we wouldn't let him come. We, ah..." Jack shoved his hands into his pockets and nodded his head toward Adam.

Adam swallowed. "Yes." He glanced down at the red leather box in his hand.

"Mama's necklace?" Holly prompted, reaching for it.

"Just a minute." Adam approached Ivy. "Over the years, whenever Holly or Laurel had an important event, they would wear your mother's diamond necklace. I don't think you've ever worn it." He looked at her questioningly.

Ivy shook her head. "It didn't seem quite right for locker rooms." She eyed the box apprehensively. In spite of the sentiment, the gaudy diamond necklace was too much for her. Three diamond strands were caught in front by a bar of three multicarat stones. From that hung a huge pear-shaped diamond drop. Once a stunningly valuable and famous piece of jewelry, her mother had gradually sold the stones to support their father's oil company and then replaced the diamonds with fakes so he wouldn't know.

Unlike Holly and Laurel, Ivy had never enjoyed the attention the necklace drew. But her sisters had worn the necklace at their weddings and assumed she would, as well. Her gown, with its low neckline, was certainly designed for it.

"Before you give her that, Adam, let's give her our present." Jack reached into his pocket and withdrew a small box.

"This is from both of us with love and our best wishes for your future happiness," Adam intoned.

"Don't be such a stuffed shirt." Jack handed her the box. "What he really means is that you've shown superior good sense by choosing Rick as your husband."

Ivy laughed and opened the box. Inside were two diamond earring studs. "Thank you both." She put them on, then leaned down and hugged them, in spite of any possible wrinkling to her dress.

"And now the necklace." Adam opened the red leather box.

Holly gasped. "What happened to the pendant? It's gone!"

"We removed it," Adam explained. He reached for the necklace and separated the top strand from the other two.

Holly gasped again. So did Laurel.

Billie's flash went off and continued flashing.

"Ivy, this is your wedding gift from Rick." Adam handed the box to Jack and fastened the single strand around Ivy's neck. Jack removed the second strand, and Adam, the third and longest.

"We've replaced the center stones with real diamonds. Merry Christmas, ladies."

The three Hall sisters squealed and two of them fell into the arms of their husbands. Ivy looked down on everyone and clutched her bouquet in frustration. "I want to see Rick," she announced, hopping off the pedestal. "And I'm not waiting any longer."

Busy admiring the necklaces, no one paid the slightest attention to her.

She swished to the door. "C'mon, Billie. You've got a wedding to cover."

"Wait!" Holly called after them belatedly. "You've got to stall until the sun comes through the windows!"

Ivy brushed her veil back. "Try and stop me." She marched from the parlor through a hallway to the narthex outside the sanctuary, enjoying the sounds of the scurrying pursuit.

Once inside the narthex, she stopped abruptly. White Christmas trees with tiny twinkling lights flanked the double doors to the sanctuary. Garlands of holly festooned the doorway, pews and altar. White silk lined the aisles. Lush strains of the famous Opus Four string quartet—they also owed Holly a favor—vibrated through the church.

But Ivy's attention was on the two dozen white Christmas trees that stood behind the altar and along the side aisles. She began to laugh, drawing the attention of the people closest to the doors. Each tree was decorated with sports ornaments. Footballs, soccer balls, baseballs, golf balls, clubs, bats, mitts and tiny helmets dangled from the trees.

Only Holly.

Ivy smiled as her sisters arrived, slightly breathless. She wound an arm around each of their waists. "Thanks."

No one could speak for several moments.

"You know," Laurel said in a shaky voice, "this might be the last time we're together for a while. Jack and I'll be in California, and you and Rick will be in New York."

"So you'll all come to Dallas for Christmas," Holly declared.

"Let's get through this Christmas first," Ivy said.

A door had opened at the side of the altar and Rick and Lincoln were now standing, waiting for her. Adam, who was to give the bride away, arrived and adjusted his bow tie. Jack blew her a kiss and led Nicholas and his nanny into the sanctuary.

At Holly's signal, Opus Four began playing a movement from Corelli's Christmas Concerto. With a final hug, Holly began walking down the aisle.

"Remember, diamonds are a girl's best friend," Laurel whispered, then followed Holly.

Yeah, baseball diamonds, Ivy thought, just before her gaze caught Rick's.

It was the first time he'd had a clear view of her, and she was delighted to recognize the same stunned expression on his face as she'd seen on Jack and Adam's. She smiled and touched the diamond at her throat. Rick grinned. The music crescendoed. Ivy linked her arm with Adam's and began walking toward Rick. Toward her future.

As she reached the end of the aisle, he held out his hand and she slipped hers into it. "You look beautiful," he whispered. Hand in hand, they climbed the altar steps.

As the minister began the ceremony, the afternoon sun peeked through the side windows. Ivy heard a collective "ah" when her veil caught the light, a light reflected in Rick's eyes.

"I love you," he mouthed.

Ivy felt her heart squeeze with a greater joy than she'd ever known. There was something magical about standing, sparkling in the sunset, with the man she loved on one side and the sisters she loved on the other.

She glanced sideways at them, noting the different expressions of happiness on their faces.

Holly's was a calm, serene happiness. With new insight, Ivy realized that in the ten years since their parents had died, Holly had never truly relaxed. She'd felt responsible for supporting them all. And she had. Even though Ivy considered herself an adult, she had been and always would be Holly's little sister. With Ivy's marriage, Holly's responsibility ended.

Laurel was truly, blissfully happy. The underlying bitterness Ivy had come to expect in Laurel's smile was gone. She had stopped blaming fate for turning their lives upside down and robbing them of their place in society. She was a hardworking and successful Hollywood agent, in partnership with the husband she loved. She was content.

Ivy had learned that each person defined her own success. To her surprise and relief, neither Holly nor Laurel had pressured her to emulate their careers. When she'd told them she planned to travel with Rick on his assignments and write free-lance articles, they had seemed genuinely glad for her.

It was a long time in coming, but it was a bona fide happy ending.

And, for Ivy, a happy beginning. She smiled up at the man at her side, the one who gazed at her with love in his eyes.

"Oh, Rick!" she blurted out, forgetting to whisper. "Merry Christmas!"

Relive the romance...
Harlequin and Silhouette
are proud to present

by Request

A program of collections of three complete novels by the most
requested authors with the most requested themes. Be sure to
look for one volume each month with three complete novels by
top name authors.

In June: **NINE MONTHS** Penny Jordan
Stella Cameron
Janice Kaiser

**Three women pregnant and alone. But a lot can
happen in nine months!**

In July: **DADDY'S** Kristin James
HOME Naomi Horton
Mary Lynn Baxter

**Daddy's Home... and his presence is long
overdue!**

In August: **FORGOTTEN** Barbara Kaye
PAST Pamela Browning
Nancy Martin

**Do you dare to create a future if you've forgotten
the past?**

Available at your favorite retail outlet.

HARLEQUIN   *Silhouette*

REQ-G